"You want more, don't you..."

It was a statement, not a question, and Ashley opened her mouth in anticipation. Beck slipped the appetizer in, staring at her lips as she chewed.

"You need dessert. I bet you don't get enough sweet things."

He was already reaching for the mango cheesecake. Ashley stopped him. "I've eaten all this food. I want you to share dessert with me." She picked up the mini cheesecake and offered it to him. He wrapped his fingers around her wrist and took a bite. Her breath quickened. She had never realized how sensuous it was to feed a man.

The last item on the plate was a fruit tart, the berries drizzled in a syrupy glaze. Ashley swiped some glaze off the top. "Try this." She offered her fingers to him.

He slowly sucked the pads of her fingers, his tongue drawing tiny circles long after every bit of food was gone.

He pulled back and painted her mouth with the sugary liquid. But instead of waiting for her to lick it off, he swooped in with the swiftness she'd seen on the field and kissed her.

It was a shocking first kiss.

This was no tentative peck on the lips...this was full-blown seduction.

Blaze

Dear Reader,

Knowing the Score started out as pure fairy tale: hardworking but financially strapped jewelry designer Ashley Craig meets handsome, rich, charming Beckett Emery. Ashley is bowled over by exciting polo tournaments, riding lessons and an exclusive polo club ball, but most of all she is bowled over by Beck Emery. A beautiful woman, a handsome man—all I had to do was write a classic romance and end it with, "And they lived happily ever after."

This was such a fun book to research—glamorous people, glitzy events, clothing and jewelry I could describe as if playing dress-up with my characters. But as I continued writing, I began to wonder just who was rescuing whom? Despite Beck's horseback riding prowess, does he really need to gallop up on his white horse to save Ashley? Or will her drive and determination save him by showing him a broader world?

In *Knowing the Score,* I'd say the prince and princess save each other. And of course they live happily ever after—they always do.

To learn more about my books and me, please visit me at www.mariedonovan.com and www.sizzlingpens.blogspot.com.

Happy reading!

Marie Donovan

Marie Donovan

KNOWING THE SCORE

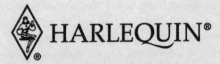

HARLEQUIN®

TORONTO • NEW YORK • LONDON
AMSTERDAM • PARIS • SYDNEY • HAMBURG
STOCKHOLM • ATHENS • TOKYO • MILAN • MADRID
PRAGUE • WARSAW • BUDAPEST • AUCKLAND

Recycling programs
for this product may
not exist in your area.

ISBN-13: 978-0-373-79534-5

KNOWING THE SCORE

ABOUT THE AUTHOR

Marie Donovan is a Chicago-area native, who got her fill of tragedies and unhappy endings by majoring in opera/vocal performance and Spanish literature. As an antidote to all that gloom, she read romance novels voraciously throughout college and graduate school.

Donovan worked for a large suburban public library for ten years as both a cataloger and a bilingual Spanish storytime presenter. She graduated magna cum laude with two bachelor's degrees from a Midwestern liberal arts university and speaks six languages. She enjoys reading, gardening and yoga.

Please visit the author's Web site at www.mariedonovan.com and also her Sizzling Pens group blog at www.sizzlingpens.blogspot.com.

Books by Marie Donovan

HARLEQUIN BLAZE
204—HER BODY OF WORK
302—HER BOOK OF PLEASURE
371—BARE NECESSITIES
403—SEX BY THE NUMBERS
470—MY SEXY GREEK SUMMER
493—HER LAST LINE OF DEFENSE

To Linda, with all my thanks for being a
wonderful colleague and even better friend.
Keep fighting the good fight!

1

ASHLEY CRAIG looked up from the glass-and-chrome jewelry case as her friend Letitia Saavedra de Léon burst into her store. Before Ashley could greet her, Tisha burst into questions.

"So? How many came? Did you get a lot of sales?" Tisha scanned the cases eagerly, her eyebrows pulling together as she saw the full stock still sitting inside.

Ashley lifted her blond hair off her neck, her shop's small air-conditioning unit no match for south Florida's heat and humidity. "Sorry, Tisha. Nobody came to the store and no sales on the Web site."

Tisha's shoulders slumped as she plopped into the pale-peach plush customer's chair, her expensive white linen pantsuit taking a beating. Ashley wasn't sure who should console whom. It was Ashley Craig Jewelry, Inc. that was struggling, but Tisha was making a herculean effort to talk up her jewelry designs among her well-to-do acquaintances.

"Why isn't your stuff selling?" Tisha demanded, brandishing her arm, which bore a white-gold bangle shaped like a dolphin with sapphire eyes. "It's gorgeous. It's unique. It should be the hottest thing out there. What's the deal?"

Ashley shrugged. "I haven't hit the tipping point yet—the one magical marketing device that will take me over the top. When I do I'll move to a new shop on Worth Drive where all the rich Palm Beach matrons can buy my wonderful jewels."

Letitia looked around the small, stuffy shop but didn't say anything. Ashley appreciated that. They both knew Ashley's problem wasn't just marketing, it was money. She sighed. "I should have picked a cheaper career. Maybe I ought to have stuck with making hemp bracelets for the surfer guys on Palm Beach Island."

Tisha made a face. "Yeah, nothing says classy like a fishy-smelling, sand-encrusted piece of wrist macramé."

"You certainly wore yours long enough." It was the first piece of jewelry she'd made for Tisha, and it had fallen to pieces eventually.

"I have the bits in my case at home."

"Really?" Ashley was touched. "Do the other pieces of jewelry make fun of it?" Tisha's husband Paolo came from a wealthy South American family and had bought her some lovely pieces, especially after Tisha gave birth to twin boys a couple of years ago.

"No, because they know my hemp bracelet will kick

their prissy asses. We working-class girls have to stick together." She patted Ashley's shoulder and Ashley squeezed her hand.

"Please don't feel bad, Tish. Word of mouth takes time, and you've done a wonderful job bragging about me around your friends, even hosting that trunk show for me. Why don't you cool it for a while? You don't want them to start avoiding you, like somebody who's trying to sell them food-storage containers or vacation time-shares."

"All right," Tisha said grudgingly, but Ashley knew her friend needed to stop acting as a commissioned saleswoman. Tisha had not been born into the jet set that Paolo's family inhabited, and she was still scrutinized for her behavior, although her adorable male heirs had gone a long way toward giving her acceptance. "But if you need any help with expenses, tell me. Paolo is generous to a fault and wouldn't care if I gave my oldest friend a hand."

"No." Her refusal came out more harshly than she intended. "No," she repeated, giving Tisha a smile she didn't quite feel. "I will be fine. There are several other ideas I haven't had a chance to try."

"If you're sure…" Tisha handed her the dolphin bracelet to put back on display.

"Positive." She came around the case to give Tisha a hug. "You are a sweetie, Tisha."

Tisha scoffed, but looked pleased. "I mean it. You let me know what I can do."

"You can kiss my godsons for me tonight at dinner." Ashley ushered Tisha toward the front door and waved as she drove away in her expensive German sedan.

Ashley flipped the lock closed. It was almost five o'clock anyway, and a storm was powering up over the horizon if she was any judge. She tucked away the jewelry into the safe in the back room and straightened the cash-register area. Unfortunately, that area hadn't gotten much action during the day—i.e., none.

She made sure the burglar alarm was set and ducked out the back door. Her shop wasn't in an awful neighborhood, but it wasn't ritzy either.

Same with her car. Compared to Tisha's German sedan, Ashley's compact car was a horse and buggy. But it got her where she needed to go, namely her apartment building.

She parked and smiled at one of the few neighbors that she knew, Mrs. Weinstein, who was out on her terrace pruning tomatoes, and who called out, "Come by for some vegetables when you change out of your work clothes." She continued clipping away, dropping leafy stems on the concrete. "It'd be a shame to get tomatoes all over your fancy blue dress, especially when it matches your eyes so well."

"I will, Mrs. Weinstein." She covered a yawn quickly.

"You work too hard, Ashley." She gestured widely with her shears. "You're a beautiful girl, and this is

Florida. I bet there are fifty handsome young men dying to meet you."

At least ten of those handsome young men were dying to meet each other, but Ashley was too polite to mention that aspect of modern dating.

Her neighbor continued, "You'd make somebody a fine wife, and he'd take good care of you."

Ashley couldn't help flinching, but hid it by pretending to swat away a bug. She made her excuses and headed upstairs, her neighbor's words echoing through her head as she tossed her mail on the white wicker table just inside the front door.

Sure, it would be easy to dress provocatively, go to the clubs where the rich guys hung out and try to lure one into "taking care of her." But that wasn't how Ashley worked. Her mother, now, that was another story…

She kicked off her white slingbacks a bit too vehemently—one crashed into the foyer wall, startling her hamster, currently the only male in her life.

"Hey, Teddy, did you miss me?" She made kissing noises at the black-and-white teddy-bear hamster in his cage. He looked at her with as much interest as a hamster was capable of and ducked into his wheel to run a few laps to nowhere. Just like Ashley.

She grimaced. *Pity, your party of one has arrived.*

Ashley gave herself a mental shake and moved through her evening routine, changing into a white knit tank top and pink boxer shorts. After she picked up some tomatoes from Mrs. Weinstein, Teddy got some hamster chow and Ashley made herself the human equivalent in the form of a microwave dinner.

She was sitting on her futon watching the jewelry segment of a cable shopping network when her phone rang. Dang, she didn't want to be envious of other people's success, but honestly, some of those items looked as though monkeys had designed them and gorillas had made them.

She answered the phone. "Hello?"

"Ash!" Tisha shouted.

Ashley jumped, spilling the pity-party potato-chip refreshments. "What's going on? Are the kids okay?"

"Fine, fine." She continued breathlessly, "Are you sitting down?"

Ashley gazed at the crumbly wreckage of her tank top and futon. "Yeah, so tell me what's going on?"

"Have you heard of Enric Bruguera?"

"Of course. He owns Bruguera Boutiques—one *is* on Worth Avenue, like we talked about earlier. They have super-popular boutiques in Palm Beach, New York, Paris, Rome..." Ashley couldn't remember where else except that no matter where a Bruguera Boutique was located, it had women flocking to wear the innovative designs.

"Bibi Herrera texted me that his boutique is helping sponsor the polo tournament at the Bella Florida Polo Club and the man himself will attend. He may even donate several pieces for the Polo Ball's silent auction."

"I'm sure they'll command a fortune." And take more

potential sales out of her pocket. On the other hand, Enric Bruguera was a household—rather mansionhold—name among the polo set and she wasn't.

"Ashley, this could be the perfect opportunity to meet him! You're the one who told me that these kinds of boutiques are supplied by various designers. Maybe he needs a new designer."

"Designers flock to him—it's not as if he posts an online help-wanted ad."

"So, flock to the man!"

"How, Tisha?"

"My husband is a rich Argentinian, Ashley. He can get me—and a guest of my choosing—into any polo tournament in the world."

Ashley imagined herself and Tisha stalking the world-famous jeweler. "Maybe we can follow him into the men's room and I can slide my portfolio under the stall door."

"Don't be silly, Ashley. The doors are full-size. You can't slide anything under them."

Ashley rolled her eyes. If that was Tisha's only objection, they were in trouble. "Tell you what—I *will* call his headquarters and ask to make an appointment with him while he is here for the tournament."

Her friend blew her a raspberry through the phone. "Not good enough. Don't you remember that old saying we learned in high-school history class? Fortune favors the bold. Calling his office and trying to get through six layers of assistants is not bold."

"Really? We learned that saying in high school?"

"*Chica,* I took it for my motto. How do you think I got the nerve to sneak into that private party after I saw Paolo going into the club? I *knew* he was the one."

Ashley remembered it a little differently, as Tisha had texted her that she had discovered the hottest ass in south Florida, and she had to see if the rest of him was just as sexy. She was saved from memory lane by an incoming call. "Hold on, Tisha, it's my store's landlord."

"Ash, I told you I'd help with your rent—"

"Hello?" Her palms started to sweat. There was no good reason her landlord should call her at home.

"Señorita Craig, I am sorry to disturb you at home, but there is a problem at your shop."

"What kind of problem, Señor Olveda?" Thoughts of robbery, vandalism and expensive mayhem struck. Her fingers bit into the plastic phone case, but she hardly noticed.

"The tobacco shop next to yours caught fire. Your shop was not damaged by the flames, fortunately."

Ashley jumped up. "I'll go right away." Her jewelry was locked in a fire-resistant safe, but if the building was severely damaged, someone could walk out with thousands of dollars in merchandise.

"Of course, of course, you need to see for yourself. The insurance company is sending men to board it up. But the larger problem is…"

"What?"

"Smoke damage," Señor Olveda added reluctantly.

"Myself, I enjoy a good cigar after dinner but when hundreds of pounds of tobacco catch fire all at once, well, it is not a good smell. In fact, the fire department called out, how do you say, the hez-met team."

She groaned. "Haz mat—hazardous materials." Great, just great. Now her shop was a public health hazard. She had visions of men in white biohazard suits stomping through her business.

"Between the smoke and the water damage from the firehoses, the insurance company says the building will be unusable for several weeks, if not a couple of months, while it is cleaned and repaired."

Frozen with horror, she couldn't say anything. A couple of months without her shop? How was she supposed to stay afloat? She skated close to the edge as it was. Maybe it wasn't as bad as he said. "I'm coming right away, Señor Olveda."

"Of course, of course. You will need to make arrangements to take your merchandise somewhere else."

She winced. Another expense—hiring security guards to transport her jewelry to rented safety-deposit boxes. Even if her business insurance reimbursed her, it would take months to get the funds. "I'll see you in a few minutes."

She rushed around, tossing on old clothes that she could throw away. Her phone rang again. Tisha had gotten tired of sitting on hold and had called again, wanting to know the dirt.

Ashley filled her in quickly.

"That's terrible! I can't believe it. What will you do?" Tisha sounded close to tears.

Ashley straightened her spine. "I'm going to stalk Enric Bruguera and slide my jewelry designs under the men's-room stall door."

2

"BECK, you son of a gun!"

Beckett Emery waved his polo mallet in salute and turned his pony to the side of the field.

His best friend, Diego Castellano, followed, cursing a blue streak in Spanish. "That pony is an old man. How can he run so fast?"

Beck patted the pony's neck. "Poor Caesar, don't listen to Diego. He's jealous because his ponies run as if they had rocks tied to their saddles." He swung his leg over the saddle and dismounted, handing Caesar to the groom to be cooled down and watered.

"Ha!" Diego dismounted, as well. "They ought to arrest you for making that pony bear your great weight. You should ride a Clydesdale."

Beck grinned. He *was* big, especially compared to many of his South American counterparts, but fortunately his six-foot-three frame didn't run to fat. "My pony knows when I'm riding him, unlike yours, who thinks a pesky fly has climbed into the saddle."

Diego's reply would never be found in any reputable Spanish-English dictionary. Beck threw an arm over his shoulders. "Come on, Diego. I'll buy you a beer in the club bar."

"Only if they have German. American beer is even more frightening than your polo-playing."

Diego lifted his beer in a toast once they were settled in the bar. *"Salud."*

Beck raised his in return. "Cheers." The Bella Florida Polo Club members-only bar was cool and quiet, a welcome change from the polo field's sticky heat. He leaned against the leather booth and sipped his beer. Diego was an inveterate gossip and Beck relaxed as he listened to him chatter away about their friends, as well as their adversaries. The bar was a masculine retreat with vintage photos of famous ponies, champion teams and even a few antique saddles mounted to the dark green walls.

"Eh, Beck, Sonja von Kasterman has been hinting that you two are getting serious."

Beck choked on his beer. "Serious about what? I've been helping her shop for polo ponies, not engagement rings."

Diego shrugged. "For some women, that is enough. I thought you would want to know. She was telling this to her girlfriends while they were here for brunch last Sunday." Diego was a big fan of the famed American all-you-can-eat buffet. Despite his smaller stature, he packed away the food.

"Hell, yeah, I want to know." He pushed his glass away, no longer thirsty. He'd thought he and Sonja were friends, evaluating ponies and attending a couple of cocktail parties together when she'd requested his company. "I've only kissed her on the cheek a couple times. How can she build a serious relationship out of that?"

"Ah, perhaps she thinks you are a gentleman who restrains his animal lusts for the sake of his lady."

Beck was startled into a loud laugh and Diego joined him. "Since when have you known me to restrain my animal lusts?"

Diego signaled for another round. "Never. That is why we get along so well."

"Well, I'll be so restrained around Sonja that the only place she'll see me is from the spectator stands at the next match." That really burned Beck. She was taking advantage of his friendship to spread rumors about them, and he didn't care for it at all.

Diego shrugged. "That is the way of women. They see us men as a trophy to capture, and once they win us, we become their stableboy to be ordered about."

"Not all women, Diego. You've met my Aunt Mimi."

"Ah, if only she were forty years younger. I would not mind being captured by her."

Beck grinned. His Aunt Mimi had been one of the

first women to play polo with men. Local legend held that she'd cut her hair and disguised her feminine appearance to play professional polo in South America for a couple of seasons before her secret was discovered. Mimi was forthright, without any ulterior motives. If only he could find a woman like her.

He glanced at Diego, who was a favorite among the club ladies. "When do you think you might settle down?"

"Settle down?" Diego's expression was puzzled, almost shocked. If Beck didn't know better, he would have thought that the English phrase was unknown to him. But for Diego, it was a philosophical question, not a linguistic one.

"Yes, as in settle down with one woman."

"Why would I want to do that?" Diego was honestly surprised. "I do not make good husband material. I am not filthy rich like you, I move from country to country throughout the year, and I always put my ponies before any woman."

"True." Diego had just described most of the polo players in the circuit.

"Now, do not go crazy on me, Beck." Diego was starting to look alarmed. "You have barely escaped one woman who wanted to put a saddle on you—do not go looking for another."

"All right, all right." Beck drained the last drops of his beer. He didn't know why he'd even introduced the topic. It wasn't as if he were lonely or anything. "We're at the start of a busy polo season, so it's not like we have time to moon over women."

"Absolutely." Diego stood, and they left the bar, passing several bikini-clad women on their way to the pool. They noticed Diego's appreciative stare and giggled. "But maybe we should not be so hasty, eh? There is more to life than polo." He blew a kiss to the sultriest beauty.

Beck tried to remember the last time he'd been on a real date, one where he'd burned for the woman, and he couldn't. Maybe that was his problem—he'd forgotten about having a life outside his sport. If he did find a woman he burned for, he'd go after her the way he played polo—with all his power, brains and skill.

"WHAT ON EARTH am I doing at a polo match?" Ashley Craig muttered. She'd never been to a match before and wished someone had told her not to wear high heels to an outdoor sport played on lush grass.

Tisha overheard her. "Trying to find Enric Bruguera so you can keep your career." Tisha was staring avidly at the polo players. "But since he's nowhere to be found, we may as well enjoy ourselves."

Ashley plucked at her dress and forced herself to look around. The men strode about like masters of all they surveyed. They wore form-fitting polo shirts—so that's where the term came from—and snug white pants untouched by mud or grass, yet. Thick leather pads covered their knees.

"*Chica,* if their polo pants were any tighter, I'd think I'd mysteriously developed X-ray vision." Tisha winked at her and Ashley gave her a small smile. She was intensely out of place among all the sleek horses and even sleeker women.

"As long as all you do is look. Paolo would not be happy if you ran off with a dashing polo player."

Tisha sighed theatrically. "I suppose it would be awkward to explain to the kids. Although they would like a pony…" She burst into laughter. Ashley had to laugh, too. Tisha's in-laws owned more horses than were at the entire polo grounds.

"As their godmother, I have to advise against your plan." Ashley settled her red straw hat more firmly on her head after a breeze kicked up. Rats, her floaty red-poppies-on-white chiffon dress was kicking up, as well. She turned slightly so the wind pressed it against her legs instead of blowing it around her thighs.

"Fine, I'll have to live vicariously through you. Maybe you can find you somebody to run off with."

Ashley snorted. "Not likely. You know I'm just here because of that fire."

"Talk about the dangers of second-hand smoke." Tisha covered her mouth. "Oh, I am so sorry—that was thoughtless."

Ashley waved her hand. "Don't worry about it. At least all my stock is safely tucked away in the bank." Tisha was right, though. The smell was almost unbearable, and the disaster-recovery-cleaning company had told her they would even need to strip the walls down to the studs and replace all the drywall.

Determined to change the subject, Tisha patted her necklace and matching bracelet. "Did you notice I wore the waterlily set you made for me a couple of years ago?"

"I did notice that. The gold looks great with your pale green dress." Ashley smiled down at her, though not as far down as usual because her shoes had sunk into the soft turf. "Why didn't you tell me to wear my ballet flats?" She bent and fussed with the grass sticking to the red patent open-toed slingbacks she'd borrowed from Tisha.

Tisha elbowed her in the ribs, nearly knocking Ashley over. "Stop messing around and look at that guy by the tent—he's checking you out."

Startled, Ashley looked up from her feet and her gaze zeroed in on the tall blond man staring at her. She straightened slowly and returned his stare. He was a good half a foot taller than her own five foot nine and was dressed in a scarlet polo shirt. His pants were white-washed onto his muscular limbs and were tucked into knee-high burnished leather riding boots. His face was lean and sculpted, with firm lips and a cleft in his chin. But his eyes were most compelling, a whiskey-brown that glittered at her. She wondered if they darkened or brightened when he was aroused. And she did want to find out.

"I think he's coming this way!" Tisha hissed, breaking

the spell the sexy stranger had woven. "Oh, my God, this is so exciting!"

"Shut up, Tisha," Ashley muttered out of the side of her mouth. Mr. Tall, Blond and Handsome was heading their way, and he interested Ashley more than any other man had in a long time.

The loudspeaker came on announcing the next match. To her crushing disappointment, the man stopped and gazed ruefully at the field. He lifted his gloved hand in a brief salute with his riding crop and joined his scarlet-clad teammates, disappearing into the crowd.

Tisha groaned. "Too bad, Ash. I thought he was going to eat you up with his eyes."

"Oh, well," Ashley replied, with a nonchalance she didn't feel. "He seemed pretty arrogant, anyway."

Her friend huffed out a breath. "That, *chica,* is called machismo. He's got something strong and powerful between his thighs, and he knows how to use it."

"Letitia!" Ashley burst into laughter.

"What? His polo pony, of course." Tisha went on tiptoe, which didn't help much. "Is his team playing next?"

Ashley craned her neck. "I think so."

Tisha caught her elbow. "Let's go watch. Men racing around on horses, their tight white booties gleaming in the sun…"

"Paolo won't know what hit him tonight."

"He knows better than to look a gift horse in the

mouth. Or a gift polo pony." Tisha shoved her into the crowd. "You're tall. Find some room in the bleachers."

After a few minutes of maneuvering, Ashley found spots for them next to a couple of older ladies. "It *is* his team." A quartet of red-shirted men on horseback trotted onto the wide grassy field. Their polo ponies had matching red leg wraps, clipped manes and braided tails. Their opponents, in blue, moved into position.

Tisha squinted. "Which one is your guy?"

"The one with the white helmet," Ashley promptly replied.

"You sure?"

"I am, yes." Somehow she knew, even from that distance.

The loudspeaker clicked on. "Playing in red, we have Team Pan-Florida, and in blue, Banque Française du Québec."

The whistle blew, and the riders charged after the ball. Ashley's player, as she thought of him, was in the thick of the action. The ponies' thundering hooves churned the well-groomed grass as they nearly crashed into each other. Her heart was in her throat as he stopped his pony on a dime in order to chase the ball and leaned at perilous angles for shots. Some of his shots were blocked, but one finally sailed between the pair of goal posts. A cheer rose from the crowd and her player raised his polo mallet in acknowledgment before focusing on defense.

Play continued for a few more minutes, and Ashley's

favorite captured the ball again. The lead player from the blue team reached across his pony to try to spoil his shot. The more knowledgeable crowd around them muttered in disapproval.

"What was that?" Ashley asked the older lady standing next to her, whose flowery pink hat sat incongruously on her close-cropped gray hair.

The woman's weatherworn face crinkled into a smile. "Cross-hook, dear. Reaching over your opponent's mount is a foul. See, the umpires are calling a penalty." The older woman's friend glared at the field, obviously too intent on the game for chit-chat. She didn't bother with a hat and wore a red shirtdress. Maybe she was a fan of the Pan-Florida team.

"Do you know the player who was fouled?" Ashley asked urgently. "The one in the white helmet."

Her neighbor laughed indulgently, glancing at her companion, who sighed. "Of course. Everyone in polo knows Beckett Emery. He's one of the best players in the world—a ten handicap, no less."

"Beckett Emery," Ashley murmured to herself, a shiver of anticipation running down her spine. The name fitted him, masculine and very aristocratic.

"His family grows the best American polo players in the world. You're in for a rare treat to watch a man like that on the field."

Tisha had overheard. "He is a rare treat, isn't he, Ashley?"

Her pithy retort to Tisha was waylaid by shouts and

curses as a blue-wrapped pony crashed into Beck's. She clutched the older lady's elbow. "Look at that! That was another foul, wasn't it?"

"Ooh, poor horse." Tisha shook her head, but all Ashley thought of was how hard the horse's rider had been jolted. He'd barely moved in the saddle, though, towering over the other players.

Their friendly neighbor stared at the field and shook her head. "No. No foul called." She turned to grin at Ashley. "Polo's not for the faint-hearted—playing it or watching it."

"Beck's tough. He can handle it, Bootsie." It was the first comment from the other woman.

A whistle blew and the players trotted to the sidelines. "Ah, the end of the chukker," the chatty woman, Bootsie, told them. "Time to change out the ponies. Two more chukkers before it's half time and we can stomp the divots." She peered at Ashley's feet and laughed. "Watch out for the manure, though. You don't want to try cleaning that off patent leather."

"Stupid shoes," Ashley grumbled. Play started again, and now that Ashley knew a bit more about the game, she was able to follow it better. Even she could tell Beckett Emery stood head and shoulders above the rest of the players—and not just because of his height. His teammates clearly deferred to him, and the other team was out to get him.

Ashley flinched with every hit he took, every daring swoop he made swinging his mallet at the ball. Before she knew it, it was half time, and they, along with the other spectators, traipsed onto the playing field to stomp the divots, which consisted of avoiding piles of manure and pressing into the ground chunks of turf the horses had kicked up. Ashley gingerly tapped one grassy clump into the ground while Tisha threw herself into it. Being a mother of twin toddlers, she was used to avoiding poop. "Come on, Ashley. Put some muscle into it!"

But Ashley stopped mid-stomp since she had spotted Beckett Emery standing on the sidelines nearby. He had removed his helmet and his fair hair was darkened with sweat, his teeth white in his dirt-streaked face as he laughed at his teammate's joke. His damp shirt outlined the lean muscles of his chest, and her heart almost stopped as he pulled his shirt free from his waistband, wiping his face. His stomach was tight enough to bounce a quarter off, and an alluring damp brown line of hair disappeared into the white trousers.

"Ashley? Ashley?" Tisha had come up beside her, her jaw dropping. "Ay, *mami, look* at him." Before Ashley could stop her, Tisha shouted across the field, "My friend thinks you're playing a great game."

Beck dropped his shirt, startled. "Me?" he pointed at himself. Tisha nodded and pointed right back. Ashley's face flamed and she gave him a weak wave.

"Your friend is a polo connoisseur?"

"Of course. Everyone says you're the best."

"They say that, do they?" His eyes crinkled with amusement.

"Of course. Ashley would love to discuss polo with you after the match. I have to meet my husband so I can't show her around." This was the first Ashley had heard of that plan. She thought Paolo was in Miami overnight on business.

"He's a lucky man." He was flirting with Tisha but his attention never left Ashley, like a laser beam.

She found her voice. "If you have time…" Good grief, she sounded all wimpy and breathy.

Beck's whiskey eyes looked into Ashley's. "I would love to meet you after the match. Meet me at the pavilion." The whistle blew, and his teammate slapped him on the shoulder.

"Good luck!" Tisha shouted. She hustled Ashley off the field, which was a good thing, since Ashley's brains and limbs had failed her after that conversation.

They returned to the stands before Ashley could put two coherent sentences together aside from, "Beck! Oh, my God! Beck! Tisha! What did you do!"

"You can thank me later," she replied smugly. "After 'later,' you can tell me all the details."

"Tisha, I can't meet him after the match. I have things to do, finish my proposal for Enric Bruguera, go feed Teddy…"

"*Por favor,* is that the best excuse you can think of? You have to feed your hamster?" Tisha sniffed in disdain. "And I happen to know you finished that design proposal three days ago. Now you put a smile on that pretty face and go out with Beckett Emery."

Their pink-hatted friend leaned around and nodded at them. "Not to butt in, girls, but men like him don't come around every week. This may be your only chance to go out with a genuine polo playboy. When I was your age, mine was named Luis. Oh, the lovely thighs on a horseman..." She stared off into space and sighed happily.

"Mine was Giovanni," her taciturn companion admitted.

"Mimi!" Bootsie was shocked. "You never mentioned any Giovanni before. And how long have we known each other? I thought his name was Juan-Carlos."

"Juan-Carlos was a couple of years later—the parliament in his country was threatening to take his throne away if he continued spending the treasury on ponies..."

Ashley and Tisha glanced sidelong at each other and giggled. Bootsie joined in, and soon they were laughing so hard, they almost missed the start of the second half. But Beck immediately captured Ashley's attention, and her heart pounded for the rest of the match.

3

"THIS IS a bathroom?" Ashley couldn't believe her eyes. With cream velvet sofas, gold-framed mirrors and black-and-white checkerboard marble on the counter and floors, the room looked more like a magazine spread of a mansion's formal parlor. The actual functioning plumbing was nowhere to be seen. If she strained her ears, she heard a flush in the distance.

"Ladies' lounge, *chica.* Everybody here pretends they have no need to use a bathroom." Tisha jerked her head in the direction of a small hallway that must have led to the sinks and toilets.

Tisha parked her in a spindly Louis Quinze reproduction (she hoped) chair in front of a mirror.

"Wow, this is the best lighting ever." Unlike most bathroom mirrors, this one didn't point out every single flaw in her skin. Considering her late nights working, that was saying something.

"A patented combo of warm and cool lighting. What's

the point in getting a facelift if the mirror wrecks it? Now let's get you touched up." Tisha whipped out some makeup from her clutch purse as she examined Ashley's face with a critical eye. Before her marriage, Tisha had been a cosmetics saleswoman at an upscale department store. Ashley sat in silence as Tisha darkened her lash-line, brightened her lids and generally gave her a sixty-second makeover.

"And now for the final touch." Tisha pulled out a red, red, *red* lipstick.

"Geez, don't you think that's kind of bright?" Ashley usually wore sheer pinks or pale rose.

"Exactly. Now hold still or you'll look like that time when we were seven and you decided we should play with my mother's makeup."

Ashley started to protest but was forced to stay silent for fear of smudges. Tisha smirked as she applied the lipstick, obviously remembering full well whose idea it had been. "Ta-dah! One sexy *mamacita* coming up."

Ashley turned, her smoky eyes widening. "Wow, this is different. You don't think the lips are too much?"

Tisha rolled her eyes. "I guarantee you that man won't think they're too much. Men love a red mouth—it reminds them of sex. Like everything else does."

Ashley gave a tentative smile. Her teeth gleamed white between her shiny glazed lips. "Okay, I'll give it a try."

"Good choice. Besides, it's super-stay lipstick and I don't have anything to remove it."

Tricked again. Whether they were seven or twenty-seven, things never changed.

Tisha's phone rang as she was stuffing her supplies into her purse. "It's Paolo." She replied in Spanish, her expression growing worried as she listened to her husband.

When she finally hung up, she turned to Ashley. "Paolo says his father is very ill at their casa in Buenos Aires. They think it's the flu, but it may be moving into pneumonia."

Ashley hugged her hard. "I'm so sorry to hear that." Paolo was devoted to his father. "When are you leaving for Argentina?"

Tisha gave her a grateful glance. "As soon as we can. The housekeeper is packing for the boys and Paolo is making arrangements with the pilots. I have to go home to throw some things into a suitcase."

"Of course." Ashley tugged her out of the bathroom and to the lobby's parking valet. Tisha gave him her stub with the promise of a hefty tip if he returned quickly. The guy took the driveway on two tires and screeched to a halt. Ashley moved to the passenger's side and reached for the handle. "I'll play with the boys while you pack, and I can catch a cab home from your house."

"Oh, no, you won't!" Tisha shook her head. "I appreciate the offer, but you are meeting that hot polo player at the pavilion and that is final." She made a shooing motion. "Go back, go back."

"But—but Tisha, this is a members-only event."

"You're my guest now and then you'll be his. If anyone gives you any trouble, tell them I'm indisposed in
the ladies' lounge. That'll shut them up." Tisha blew her
a kiss and hopped into her car. "I'll text you once we've
arrived, okay?"

"All right. Have a safe trip! Give the boys my love!"
Ashley stood in the driveway waving until the next club
member arrived in a car even fancier than Tisha's.

Not wanting to get in the way of the curious valet,
Ashley headed into the club and tried to look as if she
belonged. Without Tisha, it was a curiously vulnerable
feeling.

Her apprehension must have shown because she
was quickly stopped by a staff member. "May I help
you, miss?" The young woman in a chocolate-brown
blazer was polite but obviously had spotted her as a
pretender.

Ashley quickly put on a confident expression. "I'm
supposed to meet Mr. Beckett Emery at the pavilion."

Magic words, especially for a female. "Oh, Mr.
Emery." Her face softened for a second, but she quickly
sized up Ashley.

Ashley wondered if Beckett had many female guests
and decided that was a silly question. "The pavilion?"
she prompted.

She was quickly led to the area reserved for private
parties, a long colonnade of columns leading to a glassy
blue pool. She pasted what she hoped was a pleasant
expression on her face and took a champagne flute from

a passing waiter. The canapés looked delicious, but she feared drizzling sauce down her dress or accidentally eating a garlic puff before she had the chance to meet Beckett.

She circled the crowd's perimeter, nodding politely at whoever met her glance. It was probably a bad idea to have another glass of champagne on an empty stomach, but she hated to wander around without anything in her hands.

A buzz of activity made her ears perk. The crowd parted, and she saw him smiling and shaking hands with another man. He wore a navy-blue blazer over a gleaming white shirt and crisply pressed khaki pants. Other men wore the same outfit but looked like cruise operators who'd misplaced their ships. Beckett pulled off the look perfectly.

Ashley pressed her hand into her stomach. She was way, way, *way* out of her league with a man like him. If she ducked behind the pillar, she could get away. She'd make an appointment and approach Enric Bruguera like a civilized designer should.

But then Ashley remembered that all her cash was tied up in her inventory and she would have a hard time paying not only the rent on her shop but on her apartment as well. And to be honest, it had been a long time since she'd had the chance to meet such a hot guy. Okay, so it was since *never*. She took a deep breath. *You can do this, Ashley. Head high, smile and pretend you belong here.*

She took a big breath and casually stepped from behind the column.

Beckett targeted her as if he'd been waiting for her to appear. Ashley froze, her heart thumping wildly as his whiskey gaze bored into hers. His genial expression fell away, replaced by the intensity she had spotted as he'd played the polo match.

He easily extricated himself from the group's chit-chat and was at her side in a few short seconds. Ashley stared at him, her mouth dry.

"Hello." His voice was low and mellow.

Okay, she could manage a hello. "Hi." Okay, not quite a hello, but in the greeting family.

"Ashley, right?"

"Yes, that's right. And you're Beckett Emery?" Two sentences—that was an improvement.

"My friends call me Beck, and I hope you will, too."

"Oh. Okay, Beck." It suited him better than the more formal version of his name. "I never knew polo was so exciting. You played a great match."

"Your first time seeing one?" He smiled at her. "In that case, I'm glad we won. I would have hated to lose in front of the most beautiful woman in the stands."

Ashley's eyes widened. He certainly was the charmer. "If I see her, I'll tell her you said so."

Beck raised an appreciative eyebrow. "I can see you're not easily swayed by flattery."

"No, not really." Not until he came along.

He paused, pretending to consider his options. "How about some food? Can I sway you with some hors d'oeuvres? They have these tiny mango cheesecakes that will make you think you're lying on a beach eating fruit fresh from the tree."

"Mmm, I do like mango." She needed to eat something to balance out the champagne. Her growing sense of light-headedness had to be from that, and not Beck's intoxicating presence.

"Oh, good. If you didn't, I would have tried swaying you with alcohol." He gave her a teasing look and she had to laugh. As if a man like that had to ply women with liquor—all he had to do was arrive. He offered his arm to her, and she accepted. His bicep was rock-hard under her touch. They started toward the buffet, her filmy skirt wrapping around his trousers the way she wanted to. Slutty skirt.

At the buffet, he loaded several treats onto a plate for her while still keeping her hand firmly tucked into him. A quick nod at the waiter got them two brand-new champagne flutes, and Beck steered them out of the pavilion's light and noise.

"Where are we going?" Her heels crunched on what looked to be a crushed-shell path.

"A place where I can talk to the most beautiful woman in the polo club—and I mean you," he quickly said, forestalling any joking reply. They arrived at a small marble fountain of a water nymph surrounded by leaping dolphins. Water sprayed from the nymph's upraised hands and the dolphins' mouths. Subtle lighting illuminated the sculpture and made Ashley's fingers itch for her sketch pad.

"You like it?" He was observing her closely, his easy manner disguising a sharp intellect.

"It's gorgeous."

"And so are you." He leaned in as if he were about to kiss her. She closed her eyes in anticipation as his minty breath feathered across her cheek. But he placed the softest kiss on her forehead.

Ashley opened her eyes, trying to disguise her disappointment. He was staring at her, his own expression unreadable.

"Come, sit." Using what had to be an expensive handkerchief, he dusted off a marble bench and laid the fabric on the stone for her to sit on.

He waited until she had settled herself and bowed before her as if he were a waiter. "Mademoiselle, your dinner is served."

She had to laugh. Who was the real Beckett Emery? Charming and funny one second, serious and enigmatic the next. He sat next to her and raised his champagne flute. "To new friends."

Ashley echoed his toast, and they delicately clinked their crystal together.

"Try this." Instead of handing her the tiny slice of bread covered in chicken salad, Beck brushed it against her lips.

She took a bite, the tangy chicken and Cajun-flavored

creamy seasoning a delicious combination. "Mmmm." She couldn't help the moan that slipped from her throat.

"You want more, don't you." It was a statement, not a question, and Ashley opened her mouth in anticipation. He slipped the tidbit into her mouth, staring at her as she chewed.

After the shrimp, Beck fed her a fresh mozzarella slice topped with ripe tomato and basil, fresh cantaloupe wrapped with salty prosciutto ham and even a cold Vietnamese spring roll with crunchy cabbage and tender shrimp. "Oh, I'm starting to get full." She put her hand to her stomach in protest.

"You need dessert. I bet you don't get enough sweet things." He was right. Conscious of her weight, like other health-conscious South Floridians, she often denied herself any treats.

She started to agree, but he was already reaching for the mango cheesecake. Ashley stopped him. "I've eaten all this food. I want you to share dessert with me." She picked up the mini cheesecake and offered it to him. He wrapped his fingers around her wrist and took a bite, his gaze never leaving hers. Her breath quickened. She had never realized how sensuous it was to feed a man, to watch his lips open and receive her gift, to see his tongue dart out to catch every drop of goodness.

"Now you," he commanded. She turned the cheesecake around, deliberately putting her mouth where his had been. His grip tightened around hers and he quickly let go.

The last item on the plate was a fruit tart, the berries drizzled in a syrupy glaze. Ashley swiped some glaze off the top. "Try this." She offered her fingers to him.

He slowly sucked the pads of her fingers, his tongue drawing tiny circles long after every bit of food was gone. She fell under his spell, the warm, wet suction tugging at her nipples and lower, between her thighs.

He pulled back and painted her mouth with the sugary liquid. But instead of waiting for her to lick it off, he swooped in with the swiftness she'd seen on the field and kissed her. Although Ashley had been waiting for his kiss, been longing for it, it still overpowered her.

She clung to his shoulders as he nipped at her lower lip. She opened her mouth and he slipped his tongue inside, delicately rubbing hers. She responded eagerly, sucking on him as he took possession of her mouth in a masterful way. It was a shocking first kiss—no tentative peck on the lips, but a full-blown seduction.

He lifted his head. "I've been dying to taste you—red and juicy, sweeter than cherries."

Ashley saw her lipstick smudged on his mouth even in the dim light, and she wanted to mark him further, tell every woman that Beck Emery was *hers,* at least for a magical moment in the moonlight. She yanked him to her and darted her tongue between his lips. He opened eagerly and wrapped his arms around her.

They devoured each other, Ashley starving for the

taste of him. His mouth explored her depths, his masculine cologne rising from his smooth cheek as it slipped over her face. He smelled of leather and a slight hint of evergreen.

Ashley clung to him almost in a panic as he nibbled her earlobe, his body scorching even through their clothes. What was going on? Sure, he was a sexy man, but to totally throw her out of control with a couple of hot kisses?

His hand covered her breast and all sensible thoughts flew away as he gently cupped and squeezed her. Ashley squirmed closer to him, tacitly seeking more as she grew heavy and hot in his palm. Beck gave it to her, thumbing her breast's diamond-hard peak. He plucked and pulled at her until she wanted to scream with frustration.

She shoved her hands under his oh-so-formal preppy blue blazer to discover the primal male musculature under the fine cotton. He was hard and lean, his shoulders and back perfect specimens. She moved around to his front to that flat stomach she'd ogled on the polo field. There really was such a thing as a six-pack outside of men's fitness magazines, she discovered as she traced each muscle and sinew on his abdomen. He moaned, his breath gusting along her neck and making her shiver. His touch stilled on her while she explored his body.

She was acutely aware of his erection mere inches below her caresses, but he made no attempt to drag her hand to his zipper or to thrust against her. How did he have such self-control? Ashley was two steps away from yanking open his shirt and tossing up her skirt to get all that male heat on her.

Just as she was about to invite him to a very private party, the public party joined them.

"And this fountain is brand-new, installed only this past fall by the sculptor herself, who winters in South Florida with her Cuban-American husband…" A female voice continued, obviously giving someone a tour of what had been their secluded hideaway.

Ashley froze in horror. She'd been so transfixed on Beck, she'd failed to hear the expensive shoes crunching along the path. She shoved him away and struggled to sit up straight before the tour group arrived.

He blinked at her, lost in sensual confusion. "What?"

"People are coming!" She leaped to her feet and yanked his handkerchief free from the bench, rubbing at the red lipstick on his mouth. Darn Tisha. That sugar syrup he'd rubbed on her had obviously voided the eight-hour guarantee. He still looked pretty rosy so she tried again.

He caught her wrist. "I don't care."

"Well, I do." She scrubbed at him as if he were a sloppy toddler and then went after her own mouth. She wasn't the kind of woman who did crazy things like this, for goodness sake.

A pretty brunette in a designer dress arrived at the fountain with a dark-haired man whose interest was definitely in his companion, not the local landscaping.

"Beck? What are you doing out here in the dark?" he asked in an amused tone, knowing full well exactly what Beck had been doing.

"Hello, Diego."

Rats. They knew each other. "Well, thanks for the lovely dinner. I'll see myself out."

"Wait." Beck started to stand and sat quickly. Ashley took advantage of his aroused condition to scoot away, her body still tingling from his hands and mouth.

"Good night, Beck, it was nice to meet you." She hurried up the path toward the brightly lit, safely anonymous pavilion as nervous as if a whole herd of polo ponies was bearing down on her.

Beck watched Ashley scurry away like a skittish colt. Damn it. He would have charged after her if Diego's latest girlfriend weren't there. He didn't want to embarrass her with the khaki tent pole in his pants. Diego, of course, was impervious to embarrassment. So instead, he was stuck sitting on a marble bench with only an hors d'oeuvres plate and lipstick-covered hankie for camouflage.

"So, *querida,* Beck did not hear all about the lovely fountain."

Beck shot Diego a murderous glance, but Diego returned a merry look. Diego's companion complied, and at least her lecture had one side benefit—totally killing his arousal.

He jumped to his feet once he was presentable.

"Thank you for that information. Who thought installing a fountain was so complicated?"

Diego decided to have pity on him. "Come, dear, let us sit by the lovely fountain and enjoy its beauty in silence." He guided the woman to the bench where Beck had enjoyed kissing the beautiful and mysterious Ashley.

Enjoyed was too weak a word. Craved and filled with blind lust was more like it. If he hurried, he might catch her. "Diego, I'll see you in the stables tomorrow—but not too early."

Diego grinned and turned to the woman, obviously intending to pick up where Beck and Ashley had left off. His foot bumped into something on the ground. He bent and found a chain that gleamed in the faint light. "Is this yours, Beck?"

Beck took a closer look. It wasn't his, but he recognized the white-gold poppies linked into a bracelet. "No, but I know the lady to whom it belongs." He took the bracelet from Diego and slid it into his jacket pocket before heading to the pavilion.

"Happy hunting, eh, Beck?" Diego called. "But you may want to wash your face first. Those strawberries, they make such a mess."

Beck shook his head and wiped again at his mouth. Diego knew lipstick stains from fruit, but, as always, couldn't resist teasing. He shoved the handkerchief into his pocket and encountered the smooth, cool metal.

Under the pavilion's brighter light, he pulled the

bracelet out and examined the fine workmanship and lifelike details of the petals. His aunt Mimi's best friend Bootsie knew jewelers the way he knew horses and would be able to tell him the designer, and maybe he could learn Ashley's last name. His beautiful Cinderella hadn't left a glass slipper, but Beck would find her. He had the sneaking suspicion she would fit him perfectly.

4

"So? Did Beck kiss you?" Tisha's voice blared from her cell phone.

Ashley quickly adjusted the volume so as not to disturb the other shoppers at Pets R Us, where she was buying hamster chow and fresh bedding for Teddy. Oh, the glamorous life of a jewelry designer. One day, she was at a polo match rubbing shoulders with the rich and famous. The next, she was cleaning out a hamster cage.

"How is your father-in-law, Tisha? That is why you are in South America, right?"

"Believe me, I know that. We got in a few hours ago and this is the first chance I've had to call. He's sicker than we thought, Ashley." Her voice broke.

"Oh, honey, I'm so sorry." Ashley could sympathize. She had cried buckets when her father had left them. "How is Paolo?"

"Awful. I've never seen him cry before." Tisha sniffed loudly.

Ashley felt a pop under her fingers and realized she'd literally squeezed the stuffing out of the bag of bedding. She tucked back the fluffy paper. "Tisha, do you want me to come?" Tisha had been her rock throughout childhood and Ashley owed her more than she could say. She'd put the airplane ticket on her groaning business credit card and hope for the best.

"Absolutely not. In fact, I've been worrying about you."

"Me? Don't you have enough to worry about already?"

"Listen, if I can think about you and your problems, I don't have to think about mine. Got it?"

In a strange, twisted way of logic, Ashley did understand.

Tisha purposely brightened her voice. "So, I called the club and made arrangements for you to have a one-day pass. They're normally pretty strict about letting guests in alone without a member, but I explained our situation and that I didn't want to disappoint you or deprive you of the famed Bella Florida Polo Club hospitality due to my family emergency."

"By myself?" Look what trouble she'd gotten herself into after a short time wandering around the polo club—kissing and fondling a total stranger in the moonlight. Who knows what damage she could do in a whole day?

"Enric Bruguera will be there starting tomorrow. He swam for the Spanish Olympic team a long time ago, but they say he still likes to swim laps early in the morning. Put on your suit and lurk around the club pool. Wear some of your jewelry and see if he likes it."

Ashley looked at the bare spot on her wrist where her favorite bracelet had been, the first one she could afford to keep for herself. She'd lost it somewhere at the polo club. Maybe someone had turned it in to the lost and found. She idly wondered what else would be there. Gold cigarette lighters? A bikini top? A stray polo boot?

"Ashley?" Tisha sounded impatient. "You only have tomorrow. After that, they won't let you in until I come back. And heaven knows when that will be. Enric will certainly be gone."

"Okay, Tish, I'll do my best." She charged toward the checkout line. To-do list: clean hamster cage, feed hamster, shave her legs…boy, the fun never ended. "Give the boys and Paolo a hug for me. I'll be thinking about you."

"Thanks. Keep me posted. Okay, *un minuto,* I'll be there in a minute," she called to someone. "Gotta go, Ash. Take care." She hung up.

Poor Tisha. Ashley hoped her father-in-law got better quickly. And to think that Tisha was worrying about her despite her own problems. Ashley refused to disappoint her.

"Good morning, Beckett."

Beck winced. Served him right for answering his

phone without checking the caller ID. "Good morning, Mother." Madeline Louisa Beckett Emery had never been Mom or, God forbid, Mommy. Although she hadn't liked it when he had called his nanny Mommy.

"I hope you are well."

"Yes, thank you."

"Your aunt Mimi tells me you are in the middle of a polo tournament, which is why I didn't see you at the board meeting last week."

Ugh, the board meeting. "Yes, Mother, I just arrived a couple of days ago from Argentina and didn't have time to come to New York."

"Beckett, you are an important board member." His mother was the chairman of the financial company that her grandfather had founded. "I need you to come for moral support."

He rolled his eyes. His mother needed moral support like a shark needed fishing lessons. What she meant was, she needed his vote to steamroll the other board members. "Let me know when the next meeting is. If I can be there, I will."

She sighed. "I appreciate your hard-driving, competitive edge on the polo field, but I wish you would bring it to running our company."

Playing polo was fun—running a company where his mother wouldn't let him make any decisions was not.

"After all," she continued, "polo is a young man's game, and well…"

"Mother, you know very well polo players can play into their seventies. The horse is the one doing all the running, after all." He laughed at his joke, but as usual, she didn't. "Besides, I'm not even thirty yet."

"Beckett, by the time your father and I were thirty, we'd been married almost ten years and had you and your sister. It's been four years since you earned your MBA—plenty of time to find a suitable young woman and join our firm."

"Mother, you already have a perfectly good staff." He'd interned there for several summers and knew most of them well. If he worked there on a regular basis, he had no doubt someone would get laid off to make room for him. "Especially your upper management."

"None is an Emery." And that was that.

He made some more chit-chat with his mother, promising to come to New York for the next board meeting. "And how is Father?"

Her voice grew even more chilly. "I believe he is in St. Maarten currently."

Beck rolled his eyes. Preston Emery was an avid sailor and only left the Caribbean during hurricane season. What he did on his sailboat was his father's own business—and his mother's, too, he supposed. And his mother wondered why her son hadn't settled down?

He'd probably be the male equivalent of Aunt Mimi, happily single all his life and content to follow the polo circuit until he was too old to mount a pony. It was a life of travel and perpetual parties that he'd lived for the past several years—so why did he have a niggling sense of dissatisfaction?

THE POOL definitely looked different to Ashley at eight o'clock in the morning than it had at the party the night before. The water was an aquamarine-blue flowing over a disappearing edge in the infinity-pool style. Palm trees abutted the hidden rim so it looked as if the pool flowed into a lush jungle setting.

And it was totally empty.

Ashley looked around. Well, at least there were plenty of lounge chairs to choose from. She laid her towel down and sat on the cushion while she considered what to do. Either Enric Bruguera would come to swim, or he wouldn't. Ashley figured she'd look less conspicuous in the water, and besides, when else would she get the chance to swim in such a fantastic pool? She'd worn her sensible two-piece coral-red tankini, figuring a string bikini would negate her cover as a serious swimmer in the eyes of an Olympian.

She dived in, laughing for sheer pleasure as she surfaced. The water was perfect, cool enough to refresh but not enough to chill. She turned in a quick flip and cut through the water. As long as she had the pool to herself, she could swim laps without fear of running into anyone.

Back and forth she swam, alternating crawl with backstroke, breaststroke with butterfly. The last made her pant with exertion since she hadn't been in her apartment complex's pool in a couple of weeks. She surfaced at the pool edge with a gasp after her last butterfly lap.

Someone handed her a towel, and she gratefully wiped off her face before thanking the pool attendant.

It was Beck, sitting on his haunches. "You have good form, Ashley." The glint in his eye told her that he wasn't only talking about her swimming. He wore a lightweight white linen shirt and navy-blue swim trunks, his chest peeking out between the unbuttoned embroidered lapels. She inadvertently dropped her glance to the center seam of his trunks, which was right at her eye level. He certainly didn't seem to lack in that area either.

Her cheeks flamed and she pushed away from the poolside, gliding on her back to the middle.

He shucked off his shirt, revealing what she had caressed last night. Holy cow, if he'd taken off his shirt then, she didn't know what would have happened on that hard marble bench.

If polo didn't work out for Beck Emery, he could make his fortune as a men's underwear model. His pecs were rock-hard from all that physical activity, and that six-pack looked as good as it had felt. He was a literal golden boy, the light covering of hair glinting off his perfectly tanned skin. His navel was an intriguing outie begging her tongue to play with it.

He dived into the pool and surfaced next to her, his hair darkened to an amber-honey color, his ridiculously long eyelashes clumping together. "I'm glad I found you today." He smoothed her hair off her forehead. "You didn't even tell me your surname last night."

Ashley was surprised a cloud of steam didn't rise from her skin. Her nipples tightened under her swimsuit top. "It's Craig. And I'm glad to see you again, too."

He traced a finger across her cheekbone and down her neck. "Why did you run away?"

Ashley was having a difficult time remembering why on earth she had run away from him. She was glad the water hid her trembling as he caressed the neckline of her suit. "I don't usually make out with men two minutes after I meet them."

He threw back his head and laughed. "If it makes you feel better, neither do I."

Exasperated, she splashed water into his face and swam away. He sputtered and came after her. Her blood pounded in her veins during their chase, knowing that he was hunting her for more than a little pool-time fun. Ashley squealed as he caught her ankle.

"Gotcha, my little mermaid." He slid his hand up her calf to the super-sensitive bend of her knee, his touch arousing instead of tickling. He dragged her close to him, the inside of her thigh rubbing the side of his trunks.

"Now that you've caught me, what are you going to do with me?" She felt slightly safer teasing him, figuring he wouldn't do anything in public.

She figured wrong. He cupped her chin and kissed her. Her lips quickly opened under him, accepting his tongue as it slid along hers. He tasted minty and faintly of chlorine. She drank him in as if it had been years, not only half a day, since their last kiss. He was slickly persuasive with that wicked mouth of his, tempting her to lose her self-control in public once again.

She dug her fingers into his shoulders and hooked her leg around his waist, bringing the cradle of her thighs smack dab against him. She gasped as his erection strained against the thin nylon fabric.

Its heavy weight pushed right against her throbbing center. An involuntary moan escaped her, and her eyes flew open in shock. He stopped kissing her, his lids heavy with passion. So his whiskey-colored eyes *did* darken when he was aroused. She wondered how they would look when he came, his heavy body pinning hers as he pounded into her…she gasped again as the erotic image jolted her already-sensitized clitoris.

"You can't run away now." His usually suave voice was rough. "You feel it—you feel *me*." He pushed his erection against her and she swiveled her hips in an instinctual rhythm. He muffled a curse and pushed away from her. "I swear, if you keep looking at me like that, you and I are going to cause a scandal right here in the pool that will get our memberships revoked."

"I'm not a member." It seemed the safest way to change the subject. "I'm a guest of Letitia Saavedra de Léon, but she had to visit a sick relative, so my guest pass expires today."

He nodded. "So that's why I'd never seen you before.

I would have remembered you. I would have asked your name, asked you to lunch. Asked you to come to my bed." He added in a gritty tone, "Begged you if I had to."

Ashley swallowed hard. She wanted Beck Emery more than any man in a long time—probably ever. She'd put any kind of social life on the back burner for the past five years to build her career, which was currently at a standstill.

Suddenly she was angry at her own ambition. She was twenty-seven years old and had cheated herself out of five years of fun for something that had literally gone up in smoke. Would the legendary Enric Bruguera even show his face? Maybe. Would he be her knight in elaborately jeweled armor? Doubtful.

And when would a man like Beckett Emery come along again? Never.

"You don't have to beg."

His eyes flared with lust and he inhaled sharply. "Do you mean that?"

"I do. But not here." They were still alone but she heard women's and children's voices approaching from the changing rooms.

"Of course not." He leaned closer. "I intend to take my time with you."

"When?" she asked breathlessly.

He looked at the Roman-numeral clock above the bar. "Damn. Not now. I have to meet my teammates for practice in fifteen minutes." He swept his hair off his forehead. "Meet me at eleven o'clock. We can have lunch at the club restaurant and go for another swim at my place."

Ashley dived right in. "Can we have lunch at your place?"

He laced his fingers through hers. "I don't have much food at home."

"I'm not hungry for food."

"I think you know what I'm hungry for." He yanked her close and gave her another burning kiss before turning her loose. "Tell Señora Saavedra de Léon that she has my thanks for bringing you to the club, but that you are my guest now. I'll make arrangements with the concierge. Eat, swim, go to the spa, whatever you'd like— but be at the front desk at eleven or I'll run through the club yelling your name until they call the cops to throw me out."

She couldn't help giggling. When was the last time she giggled with a man? "I'll be there."

"Good. And I mean what I said about using the facilities here—especially the spa. My family have been members here for forty years and I doubt any of us have had a spa day more than once. I don't think we've gotten our money's worth." He grinned and swam backward as if reluctant to leave her.

"If you're sure…"

"Absolutely." He'd reached the opposite side and lifted himself out gracefully, water streaming down his shoulders into his trunks. The wet blue fabric outlined each tight buttock as if he were naked, and the newly arriving moms lusted after his ass as if it were a giant diamond solitaire.

He turned and winked at her and her cheeks heated. She watched him until he disappeared into the changing room before returning to earth. Ignoring the mommy brigade's interested stares, Ashley checked the pool for the stocky Barcelonan, but ol' Enric was nowhere to be found. The clock told her lap-swim hour was over, and she couldn't imagine he would want to swim in a pool full of screaming children.

She climbed out and toweled off, the sun drying her suit quickly. She hadn't planned on a lunch date, much less an afternoon of seduction with the sexiest man in South Florida.

Fortunately she'd packed a sundress and some jewelry in her bag. She wasn't about to go shopping in the club's ultra-pricey boutiques on his tab, but he had encouraged her to use the spa. Could they do something with her hair and makeup? She wasn't sure how much that would cost. She could always pay him back later if it cost too much. Ashley Craig was used to paying her own way.

To say Beck's mind was not on polo practice was putting it mildly. His saddle was putting uncomfortable pressure on his frustrated groin and he kept missing shots that would have been easy for a beginner. Memories of Ashley were distracting him—her sweet smile, the glint in her blue eyes, her full red lips moaning as he pressed into her burning core...dammit, there went his cock again. He'd never ridden a horse while aroused and it wasn't fun. Ashley riding him would be much more fun. He cursed and tried to concentrate.

Diego's smirks weren't helping either, especially after Beck dropped his mallet, nearly braining his teammate's pony in the process. Beck dismounted and pointed at Diego. "Not one word."

Diego held up his gloved hands in mock innocence. "If you want me to change ponies, all you have to do is ask. You do not have to give the poor creature a concussion."

Their other two teammates, who played third and fourth positions, laughed at Diego's joke as they galloped from the backfield.

"Eh, our poor Beck met a blond goddess last night and hasn't been the same since."

Beck was remounting his pony, but Diego's scarily apt statement made his boot slip from the stirrup. He landed heavily on the ground, making his teammates roar even louder.

"*Por Dios, amigo,* stay off that horse before you get hurt and can't perform for your new lady friend."

Beck flipped him a rude American gesture known worldwide, but decided Diego was right. Seducing Ashley while wearing a cast would make him an object of her pity, not her lust. And judging from their short interludes in the garden and the pool, they would have plenty of lust to burn off.

5

BECK FOUND himself pacing the lobby near the front desk. Sure, he'd left practice early, but that had only given him more time to wait until eleven o'clock. He'd hurried through his shower but had spent extra minutes on his shave, not wanting to scrape Ashley's delicate skin. He checked his dark green polo shirt for wrinkles and discreetly made sure the fly of his khaki chinos was zipped.

His wait was rewarded by the blond vision gliding toward him. She wore a buttery-yellow sundress with skinny little straps and a deep V between her breasts. God, he hoped it was one of those dresses where it was impossible to wear a bra. The skirt skimmed her hips and ended right below her knees. Three-inch sandals showed off her slim ankles.

As she got closer, he could see that she had visited the spa; her hair was expertly fluffed out and her lips were the color of a juicy peach. Her skin shimmered as if it were dusted in gold. "You look fantastic." He took her hand, not trusting himself to kiss her in public and be able to stop.

"Thanks." Her cheeks flushed and he stared at her, charmed. He didn't remember the last woman he'd met who actually blushed. "You look great yourself."

"Thanks." He guided her to the front driveway, trying not to drag her in his eagerness. "Do you still want to come to my place?" He held his breath, hoping, praying that she hadn't changed her mind.

She hesitated and his stomach flipped. "Yes."

He relaxed and got his red two-seater convertible from the valet. She ran a hand along the white leather upholstery and smiled. "Team colors?"

"Of course. If I can't ride one of my horses, I can drive this car. I love going fast."

"You're telling me," she muttered.

"You don't?" He gave her a sidelong look as he drove under the graceful palm trees arching over the long driveway.

She took a deep breath. "No, I don't. I have made plans for everything—my schooling, my business, everything…" she trailed off.

"That reminds me." He pulled her poppy bracelet from his pocket.

"My bracelet!" She took it from him and fastened it around her wrist, obviously pleased to have it back. "I never thought I'd see it again."

"It fell off at the fountain."

"Oh." She blushed again. "I'm glad you found it. It's one of my favorite pieces."

"If I didn't see you at the club, I was going to drive out to your jewelry shop to see you later today." He turned out of the club grounds and down the road leading to his townhouse.

Her eyes widened in shock. "My jewelry shop? How did you know I was the designer?"

"My aunt's friend recognized the jeweler as a certain Ashley Craig. She can't say enough good things about your work, which is beautiful. So is your Web-site photo, but it doesn't do you justice."

She slid him a sidelong look. "You are the charming one, aren't you?"

It didn't exactly sound like a compliment. "Is charming bad?"

"Not if it's backed up with substance." She gave him a challenging look.

Ouch. Well, she hadn't seen anything of him except him galloping around on his horses and splashing in the pool. Not a substantive résumé. "I have hidden depths."

ASHLEY KNEW SHE was seriously out of her depth when she saw the inside of Beck's home, an expensive villa in an exclusive gated community not far from the polo club. The outside was a creamy-tan stucco with brown Spanish tiles on the roof, typical of South Florida. Although the interior was Mediterranean-style, it was a less-fussy, more masculine design. The great room had a cathedral ceiling and a wall of windows that overlooked a slate patio with a deep blue pool. The inside was obviously planned to take second place visually to the outside, with pale marble floors and a large U-shaped sitting area of cream-colored leather sofas. The seating faced a built-in caramel armoire that probably housed some kind of giant television set. She had to smile at that evidence of single-guy living.

She clapped her free hand over her mouth. Assuming he was single… "Do you live alone?"

He smiled at her. "Is that really what you want to know?"

Darn it, he was right. "No, I need to know if you have a girlfriend, or fiancée or even a wife."

He was smiling at the beginning of her statement but the word *wife* made him flinch. "None of the above. I spent the winter in Argentina and haven't seriously dated anyone since before then." He guided her into the kitchen, outfitted with cherry cabinets and trendy nickel hardware. The appliances were stainless-steel professional grade, and skylights let in the midday light to gleam off the stone countertops.

She looked around the room. There was no evidence of any feminine touches such as flowers or even a cheerful fridge magnet and she started to relax. "Aren't you going to ask me if I'm single?"

He shook his head. "No, you're the type of woman

who is too honest to cheat." He bent and kissed her, his mouth nipping at her lips, her cheeks and her neck.

When he pulled away, she was dizzy with need. "I'd like a house tour, Beck."

"Oh, yes?" He swung her into his arms and she wrapped her arms around him. "Any rooms in particular or do I get to choose?"

"You choose." She nuzzled his neck and bit his earlobe. He shivered, causing her to bobble a bit, but she knew he wouldn't drop her.

"I pick my bedroom." He strode down a short hallway behind the kitchen and kicked open the door. Gently setting her on her feet, he continued the tour. "This is the master suite. Highlights include a king-size bed, a shower and tub more than big enough for two and French-door access to the pool, where no swimsuits are allowed."

Ashley laughed. His bedroom wore the same eggshell paint as the rest of the house with some interesting sepia photos of horses and polo matches, but the room's focus was the bed. The headboard was dark padded leather trimmed in what was mahogany and the bedding looked like pure white cotton.

She moved to stare at the pool, suddenly feeling shy. He seemed to sense this and came up behind her.

"You are so beautiful," he murmured, stroking her shoulder. "I've been thinking about you all day. I even fell off my horse because I was thinking of you."

"You did not." Although she'd only seen him on

horseback for that one match, he and his horse moved flawlessly as one.

"No, but I stumbled pretty hard. And I lost the grip of my mallet and almost knocked Diego's pony unconscious."

"Poor pony." Even if he was exaggerating, she was flattered.

"I know. I should have aimed for Diego instead."

She turned to face him. "That's a terrible thing to say."

He grinned, and his eyes crinkled at the corners. "Not if you knew Diego as well as I do. I still owe him for interrupting us at the fountain with that impromptu architectural lecture."

"I thought the fountain was pretty."

"But you're beautiful." He slipped her straps to bare first one shoulder and then the other. "A warm golden goddess for me to worship. And I *will* worship you—if you let me." He planted moist kisses on her shoulder, tracing across her collarbones to the other shoulder.

She gasped at his mouth on her skin. "Oh, I will let you."

"Good," he murmured. He pulled down the bodice of her dress and she didn't think anymore.

Kneeling in front of her, he brushed his work-hardened palm over her breast, her nipple pearling instantly. He repeated the caress on the other breast with the same effect. "You have the prettiest breasts, so round and soft. But hard here." He gently thumbed her nipples, and her legs nearly collapsed under her.

"But what am I thinking, when we have this nice soft bed behind me?" He scooped her up and laid her on the mattress. She sank into the luxurious white cotton comforter. He stripped off his polo shirt and crawled into the fluffy cocoon next to her.

She put out a tentative hand to his chest. He caught it and pressed it to him. "Go ahead. I've been dying for your hands on me."

He didn't have to ask her twice. She pushed him down and pounced. She luxuriated in his lovely smooth skin with a light dusting of honey-colored hair that darkened and narrowed in an arrow to his waistband. His muscles bunched and flexed under her touch, especially when she returned the favor and brushed his small copper-colored nipples.

He groaned. "You're driving me crazy." He moved on top of her, rubbing chest to breast, belly to belly. She unconsciously opened her legs and he settled between them.

His cock pushed into her clit and he immediately rotated his hips into her. "Oh, that feels good," she cooed, digging her heels into the bed to better push against him.

They stayed locked together that way for what seemed like forever, the barrier of their clothing only heightening Ashley's arousal. It had been so long for her, and even those flimsy memories were being burned away by the golden man in her arms.

He swiveled onto her, her nipples catching on his chest hair. Half embarrassed, half exulting and one-hundred-percent aroused, Ashley started to come, the dimly remembered tremors rising from where he moved against her belly into her breasts.

His eyes widened and she turned her face away.

"No, let me see you." He rested his elbows on either side of her cheeks and deliberately thrust hard several times, prolonging her pleasure. She finally quieted, amazed by her powerful response to semi-clothed foreplay.

He jumped up and she cried out in protest.

"Poor baby." His voice was soothing but sultry. "You're not even close to being done, are you?" He shucked his pants and navy-blue briefs and stood before her naked except for a platinum watch.

His cock stood proud and straight, jutting out from a honey-brown nest of hair. No wonder he had been uncomfortable on his saddle if that was the brute he carried around. She propped herself on her elbows and stared at him. His erection jerked under her regard, a pearl bead flowing free to coat his tip. Answering fluid dampened her panties. "Come to me, Beck." She barely recognized the purring voice that came from her throat, but Beck recognized it for the pure sensual invitation it was.

He reached for Ashley and shoved her dress down,

helping her lift her hips as he pulled it clear along with her panties. She made a vague gesture at her high-heeled backless sandals.

Beck shook his head. "Leave them on. You know what those shoes are called, don't you?"

Ashley blushed, which was silly considering she was lying naked in the bed of a man who'd made her come even with him wearing most of his clothing.

He knelt at the bed's edge, his eyes twinkling devilishly. "Say it, Ashley. What kind of shoes did you wear for me?"

"Sandals." He wasn't getting her capitulation that easily.

"No." He wedged his broad naked shoulders under her knees and nibbled the delicate skin behind them.

Ashley slumped on the bed, amazed that her knees, of all things, were an erogenous zone.

"What kind of shoes?" he asked again a couple minutes later.

"High heels."

"Not quite." He dragged his tongue north along the insides of her thighs, stopping to exhale his hot breath along the damp trail. She squealed and tried to clamp her legs together without success. "What kind of shoes?" He had drawn closer and closer to her aching center and suddenly she knew, no matter her answer, she would be the real winner of their little contest.

"Fuck-me shoes."

He growled in triumph, her answer an invitation to

what he had planned to do all along. He spread her wide and found her clit with his tongue.

Ashley panted at the hot wet pleasure of his mouth on her. He flicked her with his tongue and ran it around her opening until she went crazy with lust and grabbed his thick golden hair. He laughed, the vibrations heating her even further until he put his tongue actually inside her. She cried out as he leisurely pushed in and out as if it were his cock. She ached deep inside where he couldn't reach, where only his cock could.

"Come inside me, Beck." She yanked at his shoulders but he wouldn't budge.

He lifted his glistening face, which wore a fake expression of hurt. "I thought I was, beautiful Ashley. Doesn't this feel good?"

"Not enough," she managed to gasp.

"Do you want your poor little pussy filled, sweetheart?" He inserted one long, callused finger in her and then another.

She gasped as he stroked her inner walls, stretching and spreading her wide.

"Maybe another finger?" He slid in a third and that hit her G-spot. Her back bowed at the electric sensation and she shook as she came again.

Beck slipped his fingers in and out, building the exquisite tension. As she hit the peak, he sucked her throbbing clit between his lips, making her feel as if she'd swollen to twice the size. After that, it was a blur of hoarse screams, slick wet noises as his mouth and fingers thoroughly fucked her and the absolute knowledge that he was taking her higher than she'd ever been before.

She gradually came down to earth to see him putting on protection. She stretched her arms over her head and deliberately let her legs sprawl wide open. "Oh, *yes.*"

He sheathed himself inside her with one stroke. They both gasped, Ashley because he was so big but fitted perfectly.

Beck gritted his teeth. "I think you're still coming. You're squeezing me like crazy."

She tightened on him and he groaned. "Can't hold back any longer. Please say yes, Ash."

"Yes, Beck." She punctuated her approval by wiggling her hips.

He hooked his arms under her shoulders and was off to the races, pounding into her. His balls slapped against her bottom, her nipples erotically rubbing his chest. At first she'd been content with her previous climaxes, but the pressure built inside her.

He must have noticed her fresh arousal and bent to capture her nipple with his mouth. He hadn't played with her breasts much, and this was way beyond play. She melted underneath him as he sucked and nibbled at her, never losing a beat with his thrusts.

A cry burst from her lips and he released her breast, echoing that cry. "Ashley, Ash, oh, Ash..." He trailed off into a wordless groan as he came ferociously, his throbbing and pulsing meeting a matching reply inside her. She actually bit his slick shoulder as she exploded around him, her fuck-me heels digging into his thighs.

He collapsed onto her body, a warm and welcome weight. Gradually she peeled her arms and legs from around him and he sprawled next to her.

"Are we still in one piece?" he asked.

"I think so." She rolled onto her side and surveyed his magnificent, sweating nakedness. "Although I must say, I do admire your piece."

He gave a gasping laugh as his cock briefly flared to life. "And it admires you, sweet Ashley." He dragged her onto his chest. "*I* admire you."

She smoothed his hair away from his forehead. "You're pretty special, too, Beck."

"Good. Now that we've settled our mutual admiration, why don't you spend the day here? We'll have lunch by the pool, go for a swim, hang out."

An afternoon by the pool—didn't that sound nice? For once she couldn't remember the ten things she knew were on her to-do list—and she didn't care, either. Must have been all the sex hormones buzzing her brain. "I even have my swimsuit from this morning."

His laugh was wicked and sent shivers through body parts she thought were all shivered-out for a while. "Swimsuit? Oh, Ashley, honey, remember what I said? You *won't* need a swimsuit."

6

THE NEXT few days, Ashley *did* need a swimsuit, as she lounged by the club pool every morning in hopes of spotting Enric Bruguera. Not that poolside lounging was any sacrifice, but she had only made a couple of jewelry sales from her Web site and her insurance company was giving her the runaround as it duked out her settlement with the cigar shop's insurance company. She needed some cash flow and needed it fast. Her next option was to list some pieces for online auction, but that would be a real roll of the dice and possibly not the thing to enhance her upscale image. She could always sell them under a generic name for the money.

On the third day, her patience was rewarded by the appearance of a tanned, stocky man in swim trunks and sunglasses. Was that Enric? She had studied his Web site photo, but a man in a business suit looked much different from a man in a swimsuit, and the club was not short on tanned, stocky men.

She narrowed her eyes behind her sunglasses as he walked closer, and she spotted a distinctive cross nestled in his dark curly chest hair. If she weren't mistaken, that was similar to other items in the Bruguera jewelry collection.

Not sure how to approach him without seeming to be hitting on him, she stayed in her lounge chair. Her lack of response must have been the right reaction since he parked himself two chairs away. Right next to her would have been too obvious considering there were only a dozen people at the pool.

She lifted her sunglasses and nodded at him. "Good morning."

"Good morning." He lifted his sunglasses as well and gave her the eye. She was suddenly glad she'd worn her tank suit and not her two-piece. She wanted to audition her jewelry, not her body.

"This is a lovely pool," she commented.

He shrugged and grunted. So much for stereotypical Spanish charm. "It is pleasant now, but not when all the screaming brats arrive."

A mother with three kids was walking by and glared at him. He either didn't notice or didn't care.

Ashley gave an inward sigh. This would be harder than she thought. She examined the cross again. "Excuse me, but is that piece of jewelry from the Bruguera collection?"

He sat up straighter. "It is from that collection—my collection. I am Enric Bruguera."

She gave a little gasp, as if surprised. "I love your jewelry—it has such an exotic flair."

He smiled suavely. "Of course. We strive for the unusual and extraordinary. You have a good eye."

She took a deep breath. "Thank you. I like to think I have a good eye since I am a jewelry designer myself. Ashley Craig." She held out her hand and he briefly took it.

"Really." He dropped his sunglasses and reclined on his lounge.

Rats—she only had a limited time to pitch to him before he totally tuned her out. "If you stay longer at the club, you might see my work. My local clients are Señora Letitia Saavedra de Léon y Rodríguez and her mother-in-law, Señora Carmen Saavedra de Léon y Gomez."

He frowned at her. "You should be more discreet about your clientele."

Another misstep. "I'm sure I can rely on your discretion, Señor Bruguera. After all, we are only relaxing at the pool. It's not as if I am dragging my portfolio out of my beach bag to impose on you."

He grunted again, and she realized it was his version of laughter. "True. My assistants handle that sort of task."

"Of course." She pushed her hair out of her eyes and desperately thought of what to do next.

"Is that your work?"

"What?" Ashley was confused for a second until he

pointed impatiently at her wrist. "Oh, yes. I designed and crafted this." It was a gold bracelet designed to look like a carved stalk of bamboo.

"Let me see." He thrust out a beefy hand, and she slipped the bracelet off her wrist. He examined it closely until she thought she'd faint from nerves. "Eh, why the bamboo?"

She swallowed to moisten her mouth. "It fits in with the ecology-minded trends of the day. Bamboo is a highly renewable source of home furnishings and wood flooring."

"Gold is the most renewable resource of all."

Ashley had to agree. Give her five minutes with the right tools and she could turn this bracelet into a hundred different things.

He handed it to her. "Your other pieces are like this?"

"Yes, mostly. I also incorporate some animal designs. Dolphins seem to sell well in Florida."

"And you sell your own work?" He raised a bushy eyebrow.

"I have a small retail space—" she began, but he cut her off with an impatient gesture.

"No good. Are you a jeweler or a salesman?"

"A jeweler, of course."

"You cannot do both. You spend time selling and your work suffers. Your work suffers and you cannot sell your pieces anyway since they are no good."

Ashley sat back in the lounge chair, stunned. In his

own painfully blunt way, Enric had pinpointed her problem of the past year. Her older work sold much more quickly than the newer pieces, probably because she had had more time to craft them.

"Hey." He shrugged his broad shoulders. "I am right, no?"

She bit her lip, unwilling to admit the truth. "Maybe."

"If you say so. But me, I know the jewelry business. I own seven boutiques all around the world. I run the boutiques and you do not see me sketching necklaces or hunching over the jewelry bench. I have men to do that for me."

Ashley saw an opening. "And women?"

He pursed his lips. "Some. Women, of course, know what other women like."

"Women like my designs."

His gaze traveled to her bracelet. "So you say."

"I do." She repressed the urge to play with her bracelet.

He stared at her for what seemed like hours and rubbed his chin. "You have a portfolio."

"Of course." She clasped her hands together to keep the bamboo bracelet from trembling and giving her away.

Enric nodded. "All right. You show me your designs. No promises. I may like them, I may not. At the very least, I'll tell you what is wrong with them."

The first part made her want to cheer, the last part

made her gulp. But it was what she'd hoped and schemed. "When is convenient for you?"

"Not today. I visit my boutique in Miami later, but tomorrow I am free for lunch at Jardin des Fleurs." It was an extremely upscale French restaurant about twenty minutes away.

"That would be lovely." She gave him a business card with her phone number on it, figuring he'd already forgotten her name.

He glanced at the card. "Good. We meet at one o'clock." He stood and set his sunglasses on his chair. "And if you excuse me, I go swimming now before the children and their beach balls ruin the pool."

"I look forward to tomorrow." She gave him what she hoped was a restrained smile, instead of the insane grin she feared was about to burst loose.

He nodded and dived into the pool. She waited for a few minutes and leisurely strolled into the women's changing room. She closed herself into a curtained cubicle, hung her bag on a hook and did the happy dance of all happy dances, jumping and twirling like a maniac.

She immediately wanted to run to the polo field and tell Beck her good news, but stopped. He didn't know how embarrassingly precarious her business was or even that her store was a smoky ruin. If Enric liked her designs, she'd tell Beck and they could celebrate her success together over a bottle of champagne—her treat, for once.

* * *

"YOU'VE BEEN awfully cheerful since your swim. Did you meet anybody—mmph!" Ashley cut Beck's question off by yanking his head to hers as soon as he had closed his front door. She was indeed cheerful after her promising meeting with Enric Bruguera and was going to spread the joy to Beck.

He responded instantly, kissing her fiercely and pulling her sundress to her waist. He bore her onto his white leather couch, kneeling next to her. She gasped as he cupped her breasts, his big hands squeezing and molding them.

A faint trace of stubble pricked her nipples as he rubbed his cheek over them. "You feel great." He traced the circle of one areola. "I didn't get a good taste before." He licked her nipple and exhaled hard, the hot stream of air making her shiver.

She feathered her fingers across his pale temples, remembering how the short hair had tickled her thighs.

He grinned at her, flicking her nipple with his fingertip. "You've been thinking about me, haven't you?"

"Well…"

He sucked her deep into his mouth, pulling at her with his tongue and teeth. A lightning bolt zinged to her clitoris, but then he let go. "I want you to tell me."

She clutched him, but he shook his head, a devilish smile on his face. "Tell me, honey."

"Yes, all right! Ever since I saw you on the polo field, your big hands gripping and controlling your gear, I wondered how they'd feel on me."

"Right here?" He cupped her through her panties and she groaned. "You're dripping wet and so hot already." He licked the outer shell of her ear and caught her earlobe between his teeth.

She thrust her hips into his palm. "Have you been thinking about *me?*" She needed to know she hadn't been the only one caught in the tug of attraction.

"I couldn't breathe because I was imagining you like this."

"Oh, Beck." She helped him drag his shirt over his head and planted kisses on his brawny neck and chest. "This is crazy. We hardly know each other. We just met a few days ago."

His expression turned serious as he pulled back a bit. "Ashley, we're both old enough to know our own minds. If this seems as right to you as it does to me, why call it crazy?"

His embrace had seemed right since she'd swum into his arms at the pool. She couldn't even remember the last time she'd experienced such a wondrously scary mix of desire and tenderness. She managed a shaky laugh. "I've been a bit rusty at this." That was an understatement; she hadn't had a boyfriend since she'd been concentrating on her business.

"We'll squeak along together. Wait until you hear my joints after a lifetime of riding—I'm like the Tin Man."

This time, her laugh was genuine. He knew how to reassure her and lighten the moment all at once. And hadn't the Tin Man been a man who didn't realize how kind he was?

"Maybe I can find some oil and make you nice and loose." She massaged his flexed shoulder muscles. He was lean but extremely strong, levering his body off her with ease. There'd be time later to welcome his full weight against her. And inside her.

"I'll let you do anything as long as you wear nothing at all." He yanked her dress off, leaving her in nothing but her panties and shoes.

She unbuckled his belt and tugged his pants off. "Deal." Her hands slipped over his bottom. She loved touching his ass. It was rock-hard, with deep grooves on the sides perfect for gripping.

He thrust against her, the muscles bunching and releasing under her hands. She was even more impressed by his heavy erection, barely restrained by the thin blue-and-white-striped cotton boxers. A wave of sensual power swept over her and she nipped his collarbone, his silky chest hair tickling her cheek. "I'll do the same to you when you're moving inside me."

His breath came hard and fast as he fought for control. "Have mercy, Ashley." He shifted position so she had to release him. "Besides, a true gentleman lets the lady go first."

He dipped his finger under her satin panties. She lifted her hips and let him wiggle them off. He slid one of his wonderful fingers inside her. "You're so tight." She gasped as a second finger joined the first, slipping in and out in an easy rhythm that had her clutching his sofa cushions. He found a sensitive spot inside her and played with it.

She automatically turned her face into his pillow to muffle her moans.

"No need to be quiet, sweetheart." His fingers slowed as he smoothed her damp hair off her forehead.

She caught her breath and paused. They were alone in his house with no nosy neighbors to smirk when she saw them at the mailbox. "Touch me, Beck." He rewarded her with his thumb against her clitoris.

He balanced on one elbow and rolled her nipple between his fingers. At the same time, he leaned over her body and lowered his mouth to her other breast.

The combination of both his hands and his mouth was electrifying, her desire buzzing in a wild triangle. He swirled his tongue around her nipple, his little hums of appreciation vibrating her supersensitive skin. The man was obviously a connoisseur, tugging at her with the perfect amount of mind-blowing suction and friction.

She ran her hands along his sweat-slicked shoulders, knowing he was holding back for her sake. His thumb sped up, rubbing her clitoris in a tight circle as he twisted his fingers inside her. She groaned deep in her throat.

He lifted his head from her breast. "Louder." His eyes burned like golden flames. He licked around the curve of her breast, his stare never breaking from hers. He dragged his tongue down her sternum, dipping it into her navel.

Her whole body shook as he blew on her belly. He shifted position before she could protest and replaced his lower thumb with the tip of his tongue.

Her embarrassingly loud moan left him grinning. "That's better." He ducked his head and lapped at her clitoris, alternating the tip of his tongue with broad pressure. All the time, he kept sliding his fingers in and out. His haircut had its definite advantages, prickling the tender flesh of her inner thighs. She dug her heels into the mattress, her thighs shaking with tension. His caresses wove a shimmering web of sensation that curled from her clitoris into her vagina and finally broke deep inside her.

Startled, she tried to roll away from the powerful orgasmic surges, but he held her tight. His tongue and lips coaxed every ounce of her response. Her cries echoed through the silent house, spurring him on until she lay limp and sated.

Beck definitely knew how to use that charming mouth of his for things besides talking. And it was currently curved into an understandably smug grin as he knelt between her boneless legs.

BECK DESPERATELY NEEDED to stretch his cramping legs. He crawled next to Ashley and held her tight, his ears still ringing from her screams.

He nuzzled her silky hair, enjoying how her soft breasts pressed against his chest. Several minutes later, she stirred in his arms and caressed his jaw. "It's your turn now, Beck."

He shivered at her touch.

She rolled onto her side, her hair slipping down her back. A lazy smile drifted over her face—a smile that he had put there. He grinned like an idiot.

"Well, Beck? What are you waiting for?"

He shoved his boxers off and groaned with relief as he sprang free. He couldn't remember the last time he'd been so desperately aroused. His usually rock-steady hands shook so badly the condom slipped from his fingers.

"Come here, sweetheart." Ashley knelt and reached for the packet. He almost cried out when she wrapped her fingers around his erection. "Lie down for a minute."

He flopped onto the couch, and she moved above him, her cheeks still flushed from her orgasm. "I want to learn your body."

Without releasing him from her grip, she nuzzled his neck, licking a sensitive spot behind his ear. She moved down his body, raking her short red nails through his chest hair. She found one of his nipples and sucked it into her mouth. A blast of lightning shot from his chest to his penis.

"Do you like that, Beck?" her sultry voice hummed against his ribs.

He only nodded and squeezed his eyes closed.

"Good. I want to make you as happy as you made me." She slid her hand along his shaft. "You're dripping."

She rubbed the thick fluid around his head with her thumb.

He arched off the couch and dug his heels deep into the rug underneath. If he exploded over her hand and missed his chance to plunge into her, he'd be too embarrassed to look at himself in the mirror. He carefully detached her grip and propped himself on his elbows. "Honey, if you keep that up, I might be done before we start."

"We can't have that." She unwrapped the condom and quickly sheathed him, squealing as he flipped her over.

He braced his hands on either side of her shoulders and nudged her thighs apart. "Ready, Ashley?"

She was so damn beautiful lying under him. How he had gotten lucky enough to find such a special woman? Her blue eyes shone as she smiled at him. She nodded and hooked her smooth legs around his calves. He sank inch by inch into her welcoming softness, fighting hard for control. She was so tight, so wet, her tiny muscles clenching his erection.

She gasped his name as he thrust deeper. His chest burned from his effort not to come right away. Her plush breasts molded to him, her nipples dragging through his chest hair. "Oh, my goodness."

"You're not done yet, are you?"

She shook her head, her cheeks flushed. Her plump lips parted as her raspy breathing quickened. He reached between their bodies and circled her swollen clitoris.

She rewarded his efforts by gripping him tighter inside and out, her fingers digging into his ass.

He gritted his teeth as her hips ground against him. He increased the pace of his thrusts and caresses, not sure how much longer he could last.

She locked her legs around his waist, perspiration gilding her graceful neck and breasts. "Don't stop, Beck, don't stop." She trailed off into a long moan muffled by the heel of her hand.

"Scream for me, sweet Ashley." He slammed into her furiously as she stiffened for an instant and let out a yell of pure pleasure.

Her heavy throbbing gave him the go-ahead to loosen the reins on his self-control. He arched and drove deep inside her. Her hot, tight flesh pulsed around him, sucking him in until his sack slapped against her.

As if she'd read his mind, she lifted her hips slightly and cupped him. "Ah, God!" Her fingers teased and crazed him until he'd shoved her up the sofa into a half-sitting position against the arm. She slung her free arm around his neck and planted a deep, wet kiss on his mouth, her tongue mimicking his thrusts. He'd never felt so close to anyone. She literally had him by the balls and he loved it.

Her finger slipped behind his scrotum and teased the thread of his control. He broke off their kiss and bucked against her, her heels digging into his ass.

"That's it, that's it." She urged him on until he gritted his teeth and erupted. He groaned almost as loudly as she had, twisting and spinning inside her, around her, as her wet depths wrung him dry.

He stayed in her as long as he dared, his body shuddering from aftershocks as she showered little kisses on his cheeks and jaw. Finally he managed to withdraw and stagger to the bathroom on shaky legs. When he returned, she was pretty much where he'd left her, a glowing smile on her face.

He collapsed next to her and gasped for air as if he'd played three championship matches in a row.

"I'll be right back." She stretched luxuriously and pulled on her sundress to cover herself. Her trim backside was deliciously curved with enough jiggle to make it interesting.

She fascinated him, not just with her body, but with her quick mind and sharp sense of humor. He couldn't get enough of her. But maybe he had to work a little harder to keep *her* interested.

He jumped up from the couch and straightened the jumble they'd made. He was fixing the pillows and piling his clothes when Ashley appeared, wearing his white terry-cloth robe.

"Women would pay a lot of money for this."

"What?" He spun to face her, a pillow in front of his groin. "Pay for what?"

She sauntered toward him, a sly expression on her face as she ran a finger up his biceps and across his collarbones before circling his pec. "A hot, naked man cleaning house. I could definitely get used to this."

Beck's cock pushed into the pillow, and she noticed immediately. "Look, you even fluff the pillows."

He tossed the pillow away. "I'll fluff your pillows, Ashley." He pulled her into his arms and shoved the robe off her shoulders.

Her red lips curved into a smile and she pushed him onto the couch, ripping open a packet to sheathe him before she sank onto him, her hot, wet flesh clinging and squeezing. His eyes practically rolled back into his head. Oh, yeah. He could definitely get used to this, too.

7

ASHLEY PICKED her way through the crowd at the polo tournament quarter finals to wish Beck good luck before his match started. She spotted a dark-haired man in the team's eye-catching crimson polo shirt. "Diego?"

He turned. "Ah, it is the beautiful Señorita Ashley." He bent and kissed the back of her hand, his dark eyes twinkling. "May I persuade you to give me a real kiss for good luck?"

"No, you may not," Beck growled from behind them. "Beat it, Diego."

"You see how he talks to a valued teammate?"

"I'll let her know if I see one."

Diego groaned and clutched his chest. "And right before a match. You wound me so, Beck." He winked at Ashley and dropped her hand. "Until later, *mi bella*."

Ashley's laughter was quickly muffled by Beck's hot, hard kiss. She twined her fingers through his silky hair and eagerly accepted his display of possessive affection.

She dimly heard Diego's wolf whistle and blinked hazily when Beck raised his mouth from hers. "Time for me to go, sweetheart."

She planted another kiss on his lips. "And one more for good luck."

"As if he needs it," Diego scoffed. "Now, if you would so kindly join us, oh great and mighty Beckett…"

Beck affectionately thumped him on the shoulder and followed him through the crowd. Ashley watched until he disappeared into the stable.

"My, my, I hope my nephew can keep his mind on the match today." Beck's aunt Mimi and her friend Bootsie had walked up behind her while she was kissing Beck.

Ashley blushed. Mimi grinned and kind Bootsie took her arm. "Meem and I would like to invite you to sit with us during the match, if you didn't have any other plans."

"Oh. Thank you. I don't have any other plans for the match." Had Beck asked them to keep her company?

"Wonderful!" Bootsie gushed. Mimi was definitely not a gusher. "We have box seats and a pitcher of mimosas all reserved."

"Two pitchers," Mimi corrected.

"Even better! Now, Ashley, come tell us all about yourself."

It took the better part of a pitcher to talk about Ashley's jewelry since flatteringly enough, Bootsie actually owned some of her pieces. "My goodness, I bought that lovely yellow-diamond sunflower brooch last year. Do you have any matching pieces?"

"No, but I could make you one. What did you have in mind?"

"A ring, I think." She held out her plump hands, which boasted half a dozen rings. "A lady can never have too many rings. I should know." She turned to Mimi. "How many times have I been married?"

Without batting an eye, Mimi replied, "Are you counting the annulments?"

"Naughty." Bootsie playfully slapped her on the arm. "That only happened twice, and the third was technically bigamy on his part."

Ummm…Ashley decided a change of subject was in order. "And you, Mimi? Have you ever been married?"

Mimi shook her head and Bootsie chimed in, "She came close once, but the local bishop wouldn't marry them—said something about the heir to the throne not being allowed to marry a foreigner."

Ashley blinked. Mimi definitely had hidden depths.

"Anyhoo, water under the bridge and all that, tra-la-la." Bootsie was enjoying the mimosas a bit too much. "You must tell us all about you and Beck." She dug her elbow into Ashley's side. "Ah, if only I were twenty years younger!"

"Try thirty," muttered Mimi.

Fortunately Bootsie didn't hear. Ashley took a deep

breath. "Well, you both remember Beck and I met at the first polo match about a week ago. He and I ran into each other again at the club pool, and he asked me to lunch. We've been seeing each other regularly ever since."

"How romantic," Bootsie cooed. "And that kiss he gave you before the match—I swear, it almost made my little heart go pitter-pat and fly right out of my chest. I told myself, 'Bootsie, that boy cannot keep his hands off that pretty little blond girl and what a wonderful pair they make, both tall and fair and good-looking.' In fact, I told myself, 'Bootsie, I think our boy Beck for the first time might be—'"

"Talk to yourself later, Boots, the match is starting now." Mimi leaned forward and stared at the players lined up on their ponies.

Ashley desperately wanted Bootsie to finish her sentence about what Beck might be doing for the first time, but the object of most of her waking thoughts galloped away on his pony and the match was on.

It was worse watching him play now that she knew him, had laughed with him, had made love with him.

Ashley gasped as an opposing player's pony stumbled into his, pinning his leg between the two powerful animals. He winced but waved off any show of concern. She knotted her hands together and tried to relax into her chair. "So, Mimi, does anyone ever get seriously hurt in these matches?"

The glance between the two older women was not

reassuring. "Define *seriously*, dear," Bootsie asked kindly.

"Maimed? Paralyzed? Dead?" Ashley realized her voice was shrill and forced herself to take a breath.

"Nothing like that's happened for a good long time," Mimi said briskly. "What's more likely is that someone falls off their horse and breaks a leg or gets a concussion, and ever since they improved the helmet design, concussions are not nearly the problem they used to be." It was the longest sentence Mimi had uttered in her presence and Ashley was strangely reassured by that.

"Oh, my, yes. Most polo accidents happen when demon rum is involved." Bootsie leaned in to her. "I hate to tell tales out of school, but there was one notorious Sunday-afternoon match involving Squidgy Hopkins, six pitchers of bloody Marys at brunch and a certain wager that he could play bareback like the ancient Persians once did."

"Never laughed so hard in my life," Mimi confirmed. "Squidgy didn't feel a thing when he fell off and broke his arm. Good thing he didn't land on his liver—probably would have shattered that rock-hard organ."

Ashley burst out laughing and Mimi gave her a quick grin.

Beck swooped in and leaned off his horse so his head practically touched the ground, whacking the ball into the opposition's goal. She and Bootsie and Mimi leapt to their feet and cheered.

"What a wonderful shot," Bootsie enthused. "Our Beck always makes everything look effortless."

"He's had it too easy," Mimi announced.

"Oh, Mimi, that's not true." Bootsie looked shocked. "Beck is a very hard worker."

"I didn't say the boy was lazy, I said he's had it too easy." She ticked off her points on her fingers. "Smart, rich, charming, handsome, irresistible to the ladies..."

"Present company not excepted," Ashley murmured.

"Now, Meem, Ashley's going to get the wrong idea about Beck."

Mimi lifted an eyebrow. "Or the right idea."

Beck scored another goal and stood in his stirrups to wave to the crowd, acknowledging their applause. He spotted Ashley and blew her a quick kiss. Her heart galloped like a runaway horse and she blew him a kiss in return.

Bootsie sighed with pleasure. "A true Prince Charming. If he'd been my first husband, I never would have married the other six."

Ashley's eyebrows shot up, while Mimi shook her head. "Fortunately for us, Beck's no prince. Take it from me—princes are only good for one thing—their royal balls."

Ashley muffled a snort until she saw the twinkle in Mimi's eyes and burst out laughing. Bootsie, obviously accustomed to Mimi's sense of humor, shook her head.

"Oh, Mimi, when Ashley runs away in terror, I'm going to tattle to Beck."

Ashley patted Bootsie's hand. "Don't worry, Bootsie, I'm not going anywhere." And to her surprise, she meant it.

BECK LEAPED OFF his pony, one of Caesar's sons, and was immediately surrounded by well-wishers. He fought his way to Ashley as she descended the steps to the field. He couldn't wait for her to reach the bottom so he could pluck her into his arms.

"Beck!" She clutched his shirt, heedless of how sweaty he'd become.

"A kiss for the victor, Ash?"

"Always." She reached around his neck and gave him a hearty smooch.

Pure lust surged through his veins, already fueled by the incredible rush he always felt after winning a match. He was about ready to drag her off to the nearest private place—or public. After feeling her breasts push against him and her hot mouth under his, he wasn't feeling too picky.

Someone tugged at his arm and he frowned at Mimi, who had a hide as thick as a rhinoceros. "Beckett, the groom has a question for you about Caesar. Said he was favoring a front leg."

Damn. He couldn't delegate that responsibility and gently set Ashley down. "Bootsie and Mimi can show you the reception tent. This may take a while."

"Your pony's health comes first. Come find me at the reception tent." She squeezed his hand.

Ashley understood how much his horses meant to Beck. Short of words for once, he nodded and sent her off with his aunt and Bootsie.

Caesar was limping a bit, but Beck didn't find any evidence of a sprain or tendon pull. He lifted Caesar's hoof and found a slightly reddened spot—maybe he had caught a rock during the match. He gave the groom instructions to watch Caesar during his turnout period tomorrow and report to him afterwards.

Once his horse was settled, Beck hurried to the men's locker room. He muttered a curse as he realized he had forgotten a change of clothes since he had stayed in bed with Ashley instead of getting ready on time. Luckily he had a clean uniform, and that would have to do.

He showered and put on his fresh breeches and shirt before heading out to the party where Mimi and Bootsie were shepherding Ashley around the crowd. He'd have to remember to thank them for their kindness in looking out for her.

Mimi lifted an eyebrow at his clothing. "Did somebody schedule another match and forget to announce it or do you like to show off how good you look in your uniform?"

Ashley giggled. Leave it to his aunt to deflate Beck's ego at any opportunity. No wonder his father had retired from polo in favor of sailing—being Mimi's brother must have been exhausting.

"Thanks for showing Ashley around," he said, "but I want to show her the horses. She hasn't met them yet."

"Want us to join you?" Mimi gave him a devilish look, but Bootsie saved the day.

"Of course we won't, Beck, dear." She fanned her face. "It's so much cooler in here, and besides, the flies and the smell..."

Mimi rolled her eyes but conceded to Bootsie. Beck, realizing his narrow escape, hustled Ashley away, grabbing a champagne bottle and a pair of flutes from a waiter.

"You do look good in your breeches, you know." She smiled at him, tucking her hand into his arm.

"I would have had plenty of time to pack a change of clothes if someone hadn't distracted me this morning."

"I didn't hear you complaining when I joined you in the shower and found that bottle of body wash that made very slippery suds."

He bit back a moan at the memory of exactly how her hands had soaped him. "Ah, here we are."

She glanced at the solid wooden building. "The barn?"

"The stable," he corrected. "Barns are for cattle." He guided her into the quiet building where his precious horses were housed. Large fans cooled their stalls, which were clean and well-stocked with water and hay. He never doubted the staff for a second.

A junior groom, Juan, came out from the tack room

wiping his hands on a rag. Startled to see a team captain in the stables during the party, he stammered a greeting. "Señor Beck, what a match today! Is everything here to your satisfaction?"

"*Muy bien.* I am giving the *señorita* a tour, so you do not need to stay. Go have a drink with the men." Beck passed the groom a couple of bills and told him in Spanish to buy a round of drinks for his colleagues and not to come back for an hour or so.

Juan didn't need any encouragement and rapidly left. Beck set the flutes on a small table and opened the champagne with the quietest of pops. No need to be vulgar and startle the horses besides.

He handed a flute to Ashley and kept one for himself. She strolled down the concrete aisle, peering into each stall. "Beck, come introduce me to your friends."

He followed, not sure if she was teasing him or not. "My friends?"

"Your horses." She gestured at his ponies. "Aren't they your friends? Or are they only tools to get you from goal A to goal B?"

"Not at all," he said with indignation. "They are pampered, treasured creatures, the lifeblood of the sport."

"Well, tell me their names."

She was serious. "All right, this one is Augustinian, that one is Octavian." He pointed down the line. "And those are Claudius, Domitian, Tiberius, Hadrian and Vespasian."

"What, no Caligula or Nero?" Ashley smiled at him

over the gold rim of her glass, its metal no match for her hair.

He laughed. "No, we wouldn't do that to an innocent horse. You know your ancient Roman history. All our ponies were born and bred at a family property. It's customary to give classical names to the foals."

"So how did you escape being named Marcus Aurelius?"

He laughed. "We may be a horsy family, but at least my parents could tell me from a foal."

"They must have figured that out when you weren't running in the pasture within your first hour of life." Ashley gave him a sidelong look, her lips turned into an amused bow. She was laughing at him. No one laughed at Beckett Emery. Flattered him, courted him, seduced him, but laughed at him?

"And this lovely boy? He is a boy, isn't he?" She craned her head to peer under the horse's belly, and he stifled a grin.

"But of course. His name is Caesar, and he has sired several of these fine fellows."

"Caesar, huh? Does he bite?"

"Only if we lose a match." He plucked an apple from a bucket and handed it to Ashley. Caesar ambled over hoping for a treat. "Hey, boy, good job today."

Caesar whinnied and nuzzled his sleeve. "No, not from me—from the pretty lady." Beck showed Ashley how to hold the apple on her flat palm.

The pony delicately nibbled the fruit from her hand.

"Ooh, he tickles. Can I pet him?" At his nod, Ashley stroked the pony's muzzle. The sight of her long fingers petting the pony actually made Beck jealous. How pathetic, to be jealous of his favorite pony.

"You have a nice touch with him. Are you sure you've never been around horses before?" He ruefully noted the increasing amount of gray hair on Caesar's muzzle. Soon he would retire to a life of leisure on the family ranch.

"No, only the pony rides at the local amusement park. During the summer, if we had a little extra money, Mom would take me for an ice cream cone and a pony ride. We never really went on vacation, so it was a fantastic treat." She spoke without self-pity, her face lighting up at her fond memories. "I loved those little ponies—and they *were* ponies, unlike these full-size guys."

"Your friend Letitia is right. I do need to take you for a ride."

She nodded noncommittally, obviously not taking his invitation as sincere. Did he really appear so insincere? "A toast." He raised his champagne.

"To your win today, especially for beating that guy who crashed his pony into yours." She grinned and raised her glass.

"To you cheering me on today, which is a better victory," he responded, lightly touching his rim to hers.

She blushed slightly but didn't look away. "Cheers."

"Cheers." They both drank, her tongue darting out

to lick the bubbles off her upper lip. He caught her around the waist and captured her perfect pink mouth. She gasped but softened under his insistence, the champagne enhancing her natural sweetness.

He gently coaxed her lips open and entered her with his tongue, stroking her warm wetness. She nipped at him with her teeth, and he smiled in triumph. She always surprised him with her passion, hidden by her cool blond beauty but boiling to the surface at his touch.

He yanked her even closer, their thin clothing no barrier to the proof of his desire. Her arms went limp, and he heard champagne splatter on the floor. Without looking, he set their glasses on the table. Now they had both hands free.

He pressed kisses across her cheek and down her neck into the hollow between her breasts, inhaling deeply. She smelled of sun and lilies and her skin was as soft as the finest silk. She had only left his bed a few hours ago but he still wanted her with a surprising fierceness.

She clutched his head against her, her fingers dragging frantically through his hair. "Oh, Beck," she murmured. "Oh, yes."

She shifted, rubbing the curve of her breast along his cheek. He turned his head, capturing her nipple through the thin fabric. Her cry startled the horses as he sucked her to a peak, delicately biting her. His hand shook slightly as he cupped her other breast, and he couldn't chalk it up to fatigue from his match.

She was like a dainty peach in his hand, ripe and firm

but sweetly soft. He brushed her nipple with his thumb and it immediately peaked. She was so responsive to his touch, as if they'd been lovers for years. He knew once they joined, they would be as combustible as a lit match in dry straw. And nearly as dangerous.

He stopped kissing and fondling her and she dragged her eyes open with a questioning look. "We should stop." He reluctantly dragged his hand from her dress, and she almost pouted.

"Why?"

"Why?" It was difficult to remember why it would be a bad idea, especially when she traced the length and weight of him. "Ashley, no."

Ignoring his protests, she stroked him. "This is telling me not to stop, Beck."

He groaned and thrust into her hand before pushing her wrist away almost violently. "I want you. And you want me."

"I'm going to drag you into an empty stall right now."

He made kind of a choking noise and ran his hand over his burning face. He'd paid off the groom to have time for a romantic tour of the stables, not to make love to her over a hay bale.

"Your eyes—they're golden when you're turned on. Like molten metal setting off sparks."

That did it. "You've driven me to the edge, and now you'll see what happens when we fall over it." His nostrils flared and he crushed his mouth to hers, pressing her against the wall next to Caesar's stall. His hands traveled over her body, caressing every inch he could reach.

She eagerly met his fierce kiss, sucking on his tongue while her hands frantically worked the buttons on his shirt. She found his bare skin, and they both moaned as she pressed her hands to his chest. She explored his masculine build, teasing the nubs of his nipples, cupping his pecs. She curved her hands around his ribs, dipping into the deep valley of his spine.

Lower, lower, lower—there. She grabbed his ass with both hands, causing him to break their kiss and gasp for air as if he were some teenage boy with his first girlfriend.

She smiled in satisfaction. His eyes narrowed at her pleasure in her dominance. It was payback time. "You want to play with fire? We'll both get burned." He deliberately released her, and she whimpered in disappointment.

But his hands went to his waist as he slowly undid the buckle on his belt. Startled, she looked around. "Here?" The stables were empty, but that could easily change considering the crowds still roaming the polo grounds.

It was his turn to smile at her nervousness and call her bluff. "Why not?" She had inflamed him as a mare in heat provoked a stallion, and he swore he smelled her arousal from where he stood. She was more than will-

ing for him to take her right there, actually trembling
in anticipation.

He cast a swift look around the stable. They were
still alone, but he was sure she didn't realize security
cameras covered almost every square inch of the building. Except for one place.

He grabbed her hand and tugged her to the old tack
room. It was tucked away in the corner, unused due to
the newer and larger tack room built during the recent
expansion. He slid the door open with a creak, the smell
of leather and saddle oil a welcome scent.

"Here?" She looked around the dim room. He wasn't
sure if she had changed her mind until she grabbed him
by his undone belt and yanked him to her. Although he
loved that she had taken charge, in the stables he was
the boss. Ashley would enjoy learning that lesson.

BEFORE SHE MET Beck, Ashley had never considered
sex in a public place to be so arousing, but some dark
impulse was carrying her along into a heated vortex of
passion, and Beck was more than willing to sink with
her.

He cupped her face. "We don't have long until the
staff returns. Let's see how many times I can make you
come. Then I'll take you home and double that."

She clamped her thighs together against the tremor
that ran through her at his blatantly sexual promise.

"No, none of that." He reached under her skirt and
pulled her panties down, his hands gliding up her legs

but stopping short of where she ached for him. She stepped out of her panties and he tucked them in his pocket. "Sit." He gestured to a saddle sitting on a free-standing wooden saddle rack.

She leaned against it and he moved in close to her. "Not like that."

She gulped. He meant for her to straddle it. Naked. She stared at him.

"Never mind." He pulled out her panties, dangling the ivory silk from his fingers. "I can understand if you don't want to..." He was teasing her, daring her to wimp out.

In a fit of bravado, she hiked up her skirt and swung her leg over the saddle. She hissed out a sigh as the cool leather touched spots that had never been touched in quite that way.

A slow grin spread over Beck's face. "You've never done anything like this before, have you?" He didn't wait for an answer and moved behind her. "I told you I'd give you a riding lesson."

He pulled her skirt up to her waist. "It's important to keep your seat in the saddle. And you have a very nice seat."

She bit her lip as his fingers played with the curves of her bottom, molding and cupping them where they pressed into the saddle. The leather was rapidly heating under her and he continued relentlessly.

"Another important technique is learning how to post—that means standing in the saddle as the horse moves under you." He pushed on her butt until she lifted herself on shaking legs. When she sat, she had to stifle a scream. He had inserted his hand between her and the saddle, his fingers pressing into her clit.

"Now you tip back and forth as you become accustomed to the saddle underneath you." He gently rocked her as he stroked her clit. The leather slipped and slid under her as her juices bathed his hand. She rotated her hips, grinding against the saddle to assuage the terrible ache he was building inside her. She moved faster and faster until he pinched her clit and threw her over the edge. Tremors shot throughout her body but Beck was relentless, sliding his fingers inside her.

"That's it, move up and down on me," he coaxed her as her breath caught in a sob.

"No, it's too much."

He laughed softly and flicked his tongue over her earlobe. "Not for you, Ashley. We've just scratched the surface. Who would have thought a cool, sophisticated woman like you would sit with your bare pussy on a saddle and ride my hand?"

She moaned at both his raw words and the images they conjured.

"Clock's ticking, Ash. If my long fingers pushed inside you can't make you come again, you'll have to wait. And you don't want to wait, do you?"

She shook her head. He gently pushed on her butt. "Up and down. There you go."

His fingers spread her wide and he pressed into her

slick passage. Ashley gritted her teeth to muffle a moan when he found her G-spot. "Beck…"

"Go ahead, baby. Ride my hand like it's my cock."

She succumbed to him and rode him hard, the wet leather slapping into her bottom as he impaled her. His free hand cupped and pinched her butt, spreading her wide open and coming daringly close to her bottom hole.

He nuzzled her ear again. "Do you know how sexy it is to see you grinding your sweet little ass on that saddle? You're going to make me explode in a second."

She bit her lip and stiffened as he pushed her G-spot again. She fell to pieces on him and released a cry, her orgasm exploding into her belly and aching breasts. She slumped forward onto the saddle holder, her arms shaking.

Beck left her for a second and she heard him unzip his pants and rip open a packet. He helped her dismount from the saddle, his huge erection brushing her wet thigh. Her legs were shaking from the powerful climaxes and she wasn't sure if they would support her or even wrap around him.

He steadied her and turned her to face the saddle's side. Her scent rose from the leather and made her dizzy with the sensual memory.

He yanked her bodice down and his hands came around to cup her. He immediately plucked her nipples into diamond-hard tips. "Over." He gently pushed her so she bent at the waist. "Here, grab these for support."

He placed her hands on two wooden bars next to the saddle.

She didn't care that she was naked except for a strip of cloth at her waist, didn't care that the grooms could return at any time, didn't care that she was probably scaring the horses with her passionate moans. All she cared was that she was primed for Beck's hard, hot cock to ram inside her. She looked over her shoulder. He stood fully clothed except for his erection jutting from his riding breeches, his red polo shirt perfectly pressed and his boots shiny with polish. It was the sexiest thing she had ever seen. "If I stand over your boots with no panties on, will you be able to see me naked?"

His laugh sounded choked. "If you stand over my boots with no panties on, I guarantee I'll have you naked."

She slowly spread her legs. "How about now?"

"Now is wonderful." He moved behind her and entered her in one slick, wonderful stroke. They both groaned as he sank to the hilt. "No, *now* is wonderful."

"Mmm…" Ashley couldn't help but agree. She wiggled her bottom at him and he hissed out a breath.

"Hold on tight, baby, because I'm going to fuck you hard. You've been teasing me and now you'll find out how a stallion takes his mare." He pounded into her, his balls slapping into her bottom, his breeches rubbing her bare thighs.

"Oh, Beck," she sighed.

"So naughty. What if somebody came by and saw

me thrusting into your hot, sweet pussy? Do you want an audience?" He nipped her neck and she didn't care if he left a love bruise.

She shook her head, but her pussy clamped around him at the idea of being watched by a jealous groom or envious debutante.

He chuckled softly, obviously feeling her reaction. "You *do* want to get caught. Maybe I should slow my pace." He did, and she protested. He laughed. "Don't worry, honey. I'll cover your breasts so nobody can see them." He cupped her breasts and teased her nipples again. "And since you're bent over, all they can see is the side of your thigh." He ran a hand down her thigh and fingered her clit. "They won't be able to see this, though, or see your dripping wet little center that's the perfect home for my cock."

She writhed under him, half in anxiety, half in anticipation.

"But they'll still know exactly what we're doing. Your moans, the hot, salty scent rising off your body as you come. You can't hide anything." He moved faster in her again. "Especially not from me."

"No." Her world had shrunk to the triangle of his hands and cock. "Not from you."

"Who am I, Ashley?" His voice was hard and rough.

"Beck," she groaned.

"I'm your lover. Say it," he grated.

"My lover." She shuddered as he jerked inside her.

"Your only lover. The only man who can make you want this, make you *do* this."

"You're my only lover..." She broke off into a groan. "Oh, Beck, I need...I need..."

"You need me to fuck you." He knew exactly what she needed and took her hard against the saddle, his thrusts punctuated with grunts. She screamed as his cock bumped her deep inside and he pinched her nipples. She writhed on the leather as he milked her response for several minutes before shouting his own release. He pulsed inside her, his big body slumping over hers and his hands trapped between her and the leather.

His breath rasped in her ear and his muscles tensed. "Someone's coming." He straightened and withdrew from her body. On the theoretical side, she knew she would be horribly embarrassed to get caught naked slumped against a saddle, but on the practical side, she was too satiated and wrung out to care.

She heard him adjust his clothing and zip his breeches and he pulled her to a standing position and fixed her dress. She leaned on her elbows and smiled at him.

He laughed and shook his head. "I don't know why I bothered. You have a nice love bite here." He brushed her neck. "And that lazy, well-loved grin is a dead giveaway. You may as well wear a sign that says, 'I went riding in the stables.'"

"Ooh, sounds dirty."

He bent to drop a kiss on her mouth, his easygoing public persona such a change from the blindingly intense lover. "Oh, it was. But you don't hear me complaining."

"Me neither." She let him help her to a standing position and tucked her arm through his, as though they had stopped into the quaint little tack room for an informative tour.

Beck slid open the door and stepped into the stable aisle. A groom came toward them carrying some currycombs and brushes. He nodded respectfully to Beck and carefully avoided glancing in Ashley's direction. She was sure he guessed what they had been doing.

And the funny thing was, she didn't care. She hadn't thought of her business or her carefully crafted reputation once Beck had started touching her.

They passed his favorite pony, Caesar, who neighed. "Ah, don't fuss, buddy." Beck smiled at Ashley and tugged her close to his side. "He doesn't like sharing my affection."

Ashley's heart gave a flip. He was making light conversation, of course, after their intense interlude. She took a deep breath and reminded her acrobatic heart that that was all it was, and all it had to be.

8

ASHLEY'S PALM slipped as she grabbed the brass door handle to Jardin des Fleurs, Garden of Flowers, one of the only four-star French restaurants in south Florida and the place where Enric Bruguera would fall in love with her designs and buy them all. Maybe he would even buy some of her current inventory for resale so she could view that rarest of creatures on her spreadsheets, a positive cash flow.

The maître d' was waiting for her in the cool, quiet foyer. Ashley gave him a cheerful smile. "I'm here for a business meeting with Mr. Bruguera." She figured the maître d' knew Enric's last name.

"Ah, Mademoiselle Craig?" His fine black brows arched ever so slightly.

"Yes." She smiled and gripped her leather portfolio as the maître d' led her through a maze of snowy-white tables, and hoped her sweaty hand wouldn't leave a big, wet print on it. How would she eat anything with her stomach jumping like this? Suddenly, she wished Beck were here to lighten her mood with his sweet grin and the winks he slipped her when nobody else was looking.

But thinking of him made her feel better, perspiring palms or not. She had wanted to tell him about her meeting, but didn't want to jinx it.

"Señor Bruguera, your guest."

The holder of her business hopes and dreams stood, dressed in a fine Italian suit and a purple silk tie. "Ah, Ms. Craig. Good to see you again." He also wore a lovely tie bar of thick gold with a high-quality diamond set in the center. She bet his cufflinks matched the bar.

"And you as well, Señor Bruguera." She allowed the men to seat her and ordered a white wine. If her shaky hands got the better of her, at least the white wouldn't ruin her pale peach suit jacket and skirt. She'd chosen the color to match her jewelry, a gold lapel pin shaped like a tree with peaches made of slightly pinker gold and a matching larger peach hanging on a fine gold necklace.

The waiter brought her drink along with a sampler of appetizers—goat cheese and tomato tarts, peppered marinated olives and grilled bacon-wrapped figs. Ashley guessed Enric had already ordered and she didn't care. She was there to do business, and she doubted she'd taste much food anyway.

"So, *señor,* how are you enjoying Palm Beach?"

He inclined his head. "I make it a practice to visit

several times a year during the social seasons. I made an effort, however, to arrive during the polo club tournament. Me, I love the game, although I did not grow up playing it. My father, he was a baker in Barcelona. No horses." He lifted his shoulders in a shrug. "However, he and I, we both make the dough, eh?"

Ashley laughed and he boomed out his laughter as well. After he'd swallowed some of his hearty-looking red wine, he relaxed in the banquette and gave her an appraising glance. "You, you are born here? You have the look of someone who grew up on the beach."

"Yes, I started by making jewelry for the surfers and swimmers."

"Out of what?" He looked puzzled.

"Shells, fiber, hemp, anything I found."

"Your parents, they did not buy you supplies?"

Her mother had barely bought her enough food. "My parents were not around much." Ashley decided to tell Enric the truth about her upbringing. He might appreciate it, having risen from the working classes himself. She deliberately switched into Spanish. "My mother left and our Cuban neighbors took me in. I worked in their restaurant from the age of nine until I finished design school. Their daughter Letitia is now married to Paolo Saavedra de Léon."

His bushy black eyebrows shot up. "*Dios mío,* that thick accent tells me you are not lying." His own Barcelonan accent was as colloquial as hers.

"I am not. That is why I am driven to create jewelry—because I am starting with nothing and I want to make something, to take an ugly lump of metal and make it into beautiful things. There are too many ugly lumps and not enough beautiful things in this world."

He rolled the stem of his wineglass between his fingers and stared at her for several seconds. *"Brava, señorita.* Ugly lumps, indeed." He broke into hearty laughter again and gestured at the waiter, who arrived as if he wore jetpacks strapped to his ankles. *"Más vino, por favor."*

Ashley blew out a silent sigh of relief and allowed the waiter to top off her glass. Fortunately the first course was arriving, so she wasn't drinking on an empty stomach. She had the feeling Enric's tolerance for alcohol was much, much higher than hers.

They chatted their way through the main course, a wine-poached salmon fillet with black truffles. Despite her nervousness, she was able to appreciate the dish's exotic earthiness.

After the plates had been cleared away, she was dying to introduce their business discussion, but business in the Spanish world was not done that way. Enric was enlightened enough to talk business with her, a woman, but Spaniards did not jump into business without observing many social niceties. She knew this was as much an interview of her as a person as it was of her as a jewelry designer. Was she a person with whom Enric would want to work closely? Did she know not to wipe her mouth on the tablecloth or get slobbering drunk at business functions?

Mentally blessing Letitia's mother and father for drumming manners into her when she had been quite the heathen, Ashley smiled and discussed the weather, the polo tournament, the best beaches in the area and all sorts of trivial things before their dessert, a crème caramel that rivaled the flan Tisha's family served at their restaurant, was finished.

Enric's gaze sharpened despite his wine consumption and he stared at her lapel and neckline. Ashley knew business time was about to start. "I have never seen jewelry made into peaches before."

She understood his unspoken request and unfastened the two pieces so he could examine them.

As she figured, he turned them quickly over in his hands, knowing exactly what to look for in her crafts-manship and the quality of her materials, especially the more unusual pinkish-peach gold. "Where would we sell something like that?"

She spread her hands wide. "The home of the peach—Georgia."

He laughed. "All right. But perhaps not fancy enough for my Atlanta clientele."

"I don't see why not. It's appropriate for lunches such as ours, ladies' club meetings, even for a teenager whose mother may want to buy her high-quality jew-elry that is still age-appropriate. It's the kind of piece she can wear during college and throughout her adult years without being seen as fussy or too old. After all, a Georgia woman is never too old to be a Georgia peach." Ashley held her breath to see if Enric would take kindly to contradiction.

Instead he laughed. "Ah, and who are we to tell women they are too old for anything? Me, I am not that foolish." He handed her the golden peaches and she fastened them around her neck and onto her jacket.

Ashley thought of Beck's aunt Mimi and nodded in agreement. "Not a good way to keep your clients happy."

"And you—how would you keep our clients happy?"

He had said *our*. She hoped that was a good sign. "I believe client happiness comes as a balance—enough trendy pieces to coordinate with what's important for spring and fall collections, yet having enough classic pieces—the metal and gemstone equivalent of a string of pearls."

"Like your peaches for the Georgia peaches."

"Exactly."

He narrowed his eyes thoughtfully. "Give me your portfolio."

She complied, dying a thousand deaths as he flipped his way through the pages. Even the most professional shots were no substitute for the touch and feel of jewelry. Something that looked great on paper could be an absolute disaster in person if the craftsmanship was rough-edged, if a bracelet was unbalanced so it constantly shifted around the wrist, if earrings dragged painfully on the earlobes.

He finally raised his gaze. "I like how they look."

"Thank you." She knew it wasn't more than qualified approval.

"But…"

Ah, there it was. She'd been expecting that *but* throughout his appraisal. He would have been a fool to agree to anything without seeing the jewelry in person, and she hoped he would consent to that.

"I want my assistant Raoul to meet with us. He is the one in charge of dealing directly with the designers once I have made my decisions, and he and I both need to see more samples than your peaches. Although they are fine." He smiled at her. "You have an interesting combination of style—classic American, yet with a definite Latin-American cosmopolitan flair that might appeal to many of our clients."

"Thank you." Inwardly, Ashley was elated. Enric got it—he really did. When she sketched a design, Ashley considered what either she or Tisha liked. It looked as if she'd nailed that part of it.

"Call my office this afternoon and ask to speak to Raoul to set up a meeting. We will make arrangements for the secure transport of your jewelry."

"Wonderful." Ashley beamed at him. Yay—she didn't have to drive across Palm Beach with her jewelry case shoved under her dirty laundry and hope she didn't get carjacked.

Enric checked his unsurprisingly lovely thin gold watch. "I hate to end our lunch, but I must go to another appointment."

Ashley fell all over herself reassuring him and let him guide her out of the restaurant. "I'll be in touch with Raoul." As soon as she got to her car, she'd be on that phone.

"Remind him not to schedule it in conflict with the polo tournament. I may be traveling for business, but my accountant doesn't have to know I get a little pleasure on the side, eh?" He guffawed again.

Ashley offered her hand, and he squeezed it, surprising her by coming in for a kiss on the cheek. Despite his affectionate nature, she didn't get any sexual vibes from him, and she would know, growing up in the Latin touchy-feely culture. "Until we meet again, *señorita*." He stepped into the backseat of a shiny black livery car waiting for him and drove away.

Ashley walked very calmly around the corner, out of sight of the French restaurant, and jumped up and down in excitement. Oh, wouldn't Beck be excited for her news? But no, she couldn't tell him yet. What if Enric rejected her at their next meeting and she had to confess to Beck that she had failed? Better not say anything until her name was on a contract. Besides, she had the voice of Mama Rodríguez in the back of her head, warning her not to count her chickens before they hatched.

So first, she would dazzle Enric and his assistant, negotiate a wonderful contract and then treat Beck to the fanciest dinner he'd ever eaten. Then he would see her as his equal, someone who didn't need to scrape along, beg or borrow. Then, maybe then, she could finally *be* someone.

9

"ASHLEY? It's Beck. Do you have any plans for today?"

Not unless he counted watching her hamster run around in his purple-glitter plastic exercise ball. Oh, and waiting by the phone for Enric Bruguera's assistant Raoul to get back to her with a meeting date. Raoul had said Enric had been invited on an overnight yacht trip and would be out of touch for at least the next day. Short of renting a boat and tracking Enric, or stalking him, as the law might consider it, she was free for the day. "No, I didn't have any plans."

"My practice was canceled, so I hope you can spend the day with me."

"What did you have in mind?" She had several ideas that involved a cool swim in his pool and something hot at poolside.

"Not that." He sounded amused.

"Really?"

"All right, yes, *that,* but not yet." He cleared his throat. "Give me directions to your place and I'll pick you up."

"You don't mind coming here?" *Please mind, please mind.* Ashley looked around her apartment and grimaced. Her breakfast dishes were still on the coffee table, her clean laundry was busy wrinkling in a basket and, to top it all off, she had all of her jewelry designs and several samples scattered on her tiny dining table. Hence the dishes on the coffee table in front of the couch.

"No, in fact, I'd like to see where you live."

Oh, well, the dishes could go in the sink and the laundry basket in the closet. "Nothing fancy, but you're more than welcome."

"Great." His voice was much more cheerful. "Where do I go?"

"It's not the greatest part of town," she warned him once she'd given him her address.

He laughed. "If you saw some of the places where Diego and I hang out when we travel to South America, you wouldn't even bother warning me."

"Like to live on the edge, huh?" she teased.

"Don't you?"

She started to say, "No, of course not," and reconsidered. Since her shop had turned into the equivalent of a nine-hundred-square-foot ashtray, she had been forced to leap off one ledge after another. Or really, she had chosen to leap rather than surrender her dream. "I suppose I do." Huh. Who would have thought?

BECK FOUND her apartment building easily with his GPS unit and pulled into the spot marked for visitors. Ashley lived in a Florida-pink, older stucco building that looked to have about a dozen units. He found the front buzzer and smiled at an elderly lady watering tomatoes on her ground-floor patio. She gave him a suspicious glance until Ashley's voice came over the intercom. "Hello?"

"Hi, it's Beck."

"Come up—I'm on the third floor, apartment 3A."

The door buzzed and he climbed the stairs to the white door marked 3A.

He lifted his hand to knock and overheard her cooing at someone. "Now, Teddy, don't be like that. You have plenty to keep you busy and I won't be gone all day."

Teddy? Jealousy curled in his belly, ugly and shocking. He'd only met Ashley a few days previously. She'd obviously had a life before and would again once he left for his next tournament. But he could have sworn she had no boyfriend. Was Teddy a hopeful candidate?

Teddy was obviously giving her an earful since Beck didn't hear her reply for several seconds. "Teddy, that is enough. I don't like it when you pout. I'll take you out again when I get home."

Beck raised his hand and knocked on her door.

"Just a minute," she called. He sensed her checking the peephole and heard her open several locks.

"Beck!" She gave him a welcome smile. He searched for any hint of nervousness or guilt and found none.

"Hi, Ashley." He gave her a kiss. "I heard you talking to Teddy." Better to get it out in the open instead of stewing about it.

"Oh. You heard that?" She did look embarrassed and his heart sank. He even took a casual glance around her apartment for signs of male inhabitants, but couldn't find any.

"I suppose I should introduce you two, but I have to tell you, Teddy doesn't like men."

Didn't like the competition, huh?

He squared his shoulders. "Is Teddy here right now?"

She gave him a weird look. "Sure. Where else would he be? He lives with me."

Oh, shit. Beck couldn't believe how much that hurt. "I think the three of us should have a little chat."

Ashley bit her lip. "I don't know if he'll have much to say."

"Well, I definitely do."

"If you insist." Her mouth pressed into a tight line, Ashley walked into her living room. Despite Beck's growing unease, he couldn't help noticing how her hips swayed under her mint-green dress. Beck looked around, but there was nobody sitting on her white couch. She stopped at a small yellow-metal cage sitting on a white wicker table.

"Teddy?" She tapped the bars. "Come here, sweet

pea." A roly-poly black-and-white rodent waddled out from a small cardboard box set in the cage and grabbed the bars with two tiny pink paws. Ashley sprang the latch and lifted Teddy into her hands, nuzzling his fur. "Who's my good boy, huh?"

"He's Teddy?" Beck hadn't had that same wind-knocked-out feeling since he'd last fallen off his horse.

"I'd let you hold him, but as I said before, Teddy doesn't like men." She broke into a wide grin. "He's also somewhat taciturn." What Beck had mistaken for anxiety had actually been Ashley trying not to laugh her ass off at him.

My, my, wasn't Beckett Winston Emery quite the macho man? Jealous of a freaking hamster. And a teddy-bear hamster, no less. "Oh, go ahead and laugh," he said crossly.

She burst into laughter, the hamster bouncing in her hands. She plopped him into a purple plastic ball and he immediately ran away, probably to get away from the large grumpy male human.

"Oh, Beck, the look on your face. I don't know whether to be flattered or insulted that you think I have men crawling out of the woodwork."

He grimaced. "I am sorry." She'd already said she wasn't seeing other men, and she'd never done anything to indicate differently. "I...don't know what else to say." He rubbed his face.

She gave him a considering look. "What kind of women have you known, Beckett Emery?"

Her question immediately triggered images of certain women from his past. Lucia, the Argentinian woman who hadn't told him she'd been engaged to a family friend practically since birth. Inga, who had claimed she and her husband had an "open" marriage—the husband Beck hadn't known about until after he'd slept with Inga. Diana, who had slipped into Diego's hotel room in Montevideo wearing nothing but a silk robe and a smile after Beck had unexpectedly been called back to the States for a family crisis. Even Diego, not particularly known for his sexual reticence, had been offended on his behalf and booted her into the hall.

"I see."

He jolted to the present, realizing Ashley was staring at him thoughtfully. "I…I…"

"The rich are different from you and me. Well, me, anyway."

"I'm sorry," he repeated.

She waved a hand. "We are all products of our experience. As for me, Teddy is the only male I can really trust."

Beck jumped slightly as the hamster ball clattered onto the kitchen tiles. "Why?"

"You don't want to know." She turned her back to him and followed Teddy.

"What if I do want to know?"

She turned to face him, her blue eyes hard for the

first time since they'd met. "Okay. My father left us when I was six and my mother spent a couple of years auditioning replacements before taking off with one of them when I was nine."

Beck winced. "Who raised you?"

"Letitia's parents. We lived in the same building and they took me in—even going through the adoption application so it could be official. Otherwise I would have been sent to live with strangers."

He pulled her into his arms. His own mother might have been a tad rigid in her child-raising beliefs, but a strong sense of duty had accompanied those beliefs. "Where is your mother now?"

She shrugged. "She contacted me again when I was a teenager but I was happy with Letitia and her family."

Beck noticed how Ashley didn't refer to them as her own family.

"My mother remarried a few years ago and lives in Jacksonville. Her new husband is a retired accountant and is completely dazzled by her, so they get along fine."

"You dazzle me, Ashley." He brushed his lips over hers. "To come out of a childhood like yours as kind and good as you are…"

She shook her head. "Don't put me on a pedestal, Beck. I don't deserve that."

Yes, she did, but he wouldn't press the point, sensing she wanted to change the subject. She followed

Teddy into the kitchen. "Would you like something to drink?"

"Oh, um…" He was having a hard time thinking straight as the revelations about her dreadful childhood churned in his head. "How about some water?"

She poked her head around the corner. "Beck, you daredevil, you. Do you want to be really reckless and have some ice cubes?"

Moving quickly, he grabbed her around the waist and growled into her neck. She giggled and swatted at him. "If you give me any ice cubes, I'll drop them down your shirt. What say you tuck Teddy in his hut and go put on some jeans?"

"Jeans?" She made a face. "It's too hot for jeans." She was wearing one of the pretty sundresses that flattered her blond hair and tanned shoulders.

"Jeans," he repeated. "And a pair of good sturdy shoes." Like practically every other woman in south Florida, she was wearing flip-flops.

She gave him a suspicious stare. "Did your groom quit and you need me to clean your stables?"

He caught her wrists. "Would I do that to your pretty hands?"

Instead of oohing at his compliment, she laughed again. "Have you looked at my hands lately?"

Of course he had—her hands as they moved over his chest, his belly, his back…he was getting distracted by happy memories and certain parts of him were getting happy, too. He took a deep breath.

"Here's a burn scar from my soldering iron, here's a puncture wound where a wire went about an inch deep into my thumb, and various dings and scratches."

He obediently checked and did see some lighter marks, but they only enhanced her instead of marring her. "If we're comparing scars, here's where I had pins put in my wrist after I fell off my pony, here's where my thumbnail fell off after a pony crushed my hand between its rump and the stable wall." He didn't mention the various fractured fingers and a couple of concussions that would have split his head open if he hadn't been wearing his helmet. Anything that involved large mammals running at high speed was high risk; at least the sport no longer used enemies' severed heads as polo balls.

"I guess we all have our scars, don't we?" She gave him a sad smile, and he wanted to wrap her in his arms to keep anything bad from ever happening to her again.

"Jeans." He knew she would push him away if he tried to comfort her, so he winked at her and nodded at the hallway presumably leading to her bedroom.

"Fine." She stashed Teddy in his cage and headed down the hall.

He wandered to the hamster hut and eyeballed the little rodent, who bared his surprisingly large teeth. "So, Teddy, I guess you and I will have to look after Ashley, huh?"

The hamster scurried into his little den, leaving Beck talking to thin, cedar-scented air.

"Slacker. I guess it'll be just me." Beck waited for the cold chill to run along his spine, and when it didn't, he shrugged. "Beck and Ashley." He grinned to himself. That had a nice ring to it.

"AHA! You *are* going to make me clean the stables." Ashley purposely injected cheer into her voice as Beck pulled up to a stable, its long ivory-colored building gleaming in the sun. White fences extended from each end and Ashley spotted several horses grazing in the morning sun. There was an ebony-black mother and her foal, the foal kicking its hooves as it played in the thick green grass.

"Good exercise. Even us rich guys grow up shoveling manure with the best of them. Besides, I'm taking you for a ride. Since you're a guest, I won't make you do stable chores. Mimi manages the place and believe me, her stable hands work hard."

"Beck, I've only been on a horse a couple times. I don't think I can manage the kind of horse you're used to."

He kissed the tip of her nose. "Trust me." He jumped out of the truck and opened the door for her. "I haven't lost a student yet."

She took his hand and climbed out. Again with the trust thing. He guided her across the gravel parking lot and into the stable. It was smaller than the facility at the polo club, but just as clean and well-maintained.

Ashley heard the voices of children. "Oh, so you give children lessons, too?" They probably had some tamer horses as well.

"Children and adults both. Mimi and I adapt the lessons as needed."

"Oh, right." She didn't understand what he really meant until she saw a woman pushing a boy in a wheelchair, and an older girl with Down syndrome following her dad, she assumed. "Oh," she said in surprise. *"Oh."*

She stared at Beck. He gave her a small smile and waited for her reaction to the children. Again she wondered what kind of woman he was used to. Someone who had been repulsed by the sweet little faces in front of her? Someone who had thought it was a waste of time for a highly skilled polo player to teach riding to disabled children?

That kind of woman was a serious bitch.

"I think this is a lovely idea. The kids must really enjoy being up so high on the horses."

He immediately relaxed and grinned. "Oh, they do."

Ashley relaxed, too. She had passed an important test by approving of Beck's volunteer work. And how could she not? The stable hand pushed the boy's wheelchair up a ramp next to which a spotted pony waited patiently, held in place by a woman riding instructor.

The boy let out a brief howl, but was quickly soothed by the stable hand. His mother stood to the side, giving him a brave smile, but Ashley could see her white knuckles from where she stood.

They settled the boy into a complicated saddle on top of the pony and guided him into a slow walk. His panicked expression was quickly replaced by sheer elation. "Mom! Look!" His speech was harsh but his joy was unmistakable.

Ashley grabbed Beck's hand and held on tight. "This is a great thing to do. Are you a donor, too?"

"Donor?" His aunt Mimi passing by overheard her question. "This is Beck's baby. He convinced me to ask everybody we knew for funding to build the stable, find decent ponies and hire staff who are experienced in therapeutic riding. Despite all his hard work, he won't let me give him any credit for it."

"When you first heard about my idea, you said it was a waste of time."

"That was before I saw what good it does." Mimi sniffed. "I was wrong, and I'm woman enough to admit it. Riding a horse for these kids—well, it's something magical."

"Magical," Ashley echoed, seeing the brilliant smile on the boy's face as he ambled around the ring. To be physically constrained almost every minute of your life, and then lifted free from your boundaries high into the air, the master of a powerful animal and the master of your own destiny, even for a short time, must be wonderful.

And it was Beck who had seen the simple magic in riding a horse. She flung her arms around his neck and kissed his cheek. "You knew, didn't you? How much this would mean to them. And their families." The gentle sniffling of the boy's mom echoed through the stable.

Surprised by her affectionate onslaught, Beck patted her back. "Oh, hey, anyone would have done it. We'd been talking for years about doing something like this."

Mimi gave a loud snort. "Yeah, but you were the only one who got off your ass and did it."

He shrugged. Ashley took a deep breath and kissed him on the mouth. His lips pulled into a smile and he returned her kiss.

The kiss went on and Ashley overheard Mimi clear her throat. "Ah, young love. Now cut it out."

Ashley jerked back and stared into Beck's eyes. He looked as startled as she felt. Love? She quickly stepped away, unwilling to glance again in his direction.

Mimi slapped Beck on the shoulder and caught sight of a stable hand who was slacking off. "Hey, is that what I told you to do?" She stomped off and left them standing there awkwardly.

Beck broke the silence first. "Come meet the horse I picked for you."

"Oh, okay." She trailed behind him as he stopped in front of a big black horse.

"This here is Widowmaker," he said in a thick drawl.

"What?"

"Just kidding. His name is Dodger, and he's as gentle as they come."

"But he's so *big*." She couldn't help a bit of nervousness.

"You're tall, honey. If I put you on a smaller horse, your feet might drag on the ground."

"If you're sure…"

He turned her to face him. "Ashley, I would never let anything happen to you. You believe me, don't you?"

Warmth swelled in her chest.

"Good." After fitting them with riding helmets, he showed her how to put her foot into the stirrup and boosted her into the saddle, his hands cupping her butt.

She grinned down at him for once. "Do you help everybody onto their horse in that way?"

He grinned back. "Only Diego."

Ashley burst into laughter, making her horse shuffle sideways and swish its tail. She froze and he chuckled.

"Just brushing away some flies, honey." He patted her calf, the muscle already protesting from the unfamiliar position. The stablehand had brought out a big black horse for Beck, who vaulted into the saddle with his customary grace.

"What's the name of your horse?" The animal snorted and danced as Beck quickly brought it under control.

"Diablo."

She laughed at his joke. Devil, indeed. "No, really."

"Yes, really. He's pure devil. I don't think anybody's told him he's not a stallion anymore."

"Oh." To emphasize his badass reputation, Diablo reared up on his hind legs. Ashley gasped, but Beck easily pulled him back down.

"Ash, he needs to run off some steam. I'll take him around the ring a few times." He gestured to the stablehand, who took Dodger's bridle so he wouldn't follow.

Beck guided Diablo to the ring, where Mimi opened the gate for him. "Run the sass out of that boy, Beck. He tried to bite Javier twice today."

The stablehand who held Dodger muttered a Spanish imprecation against the feisty horse. Ashley giggled and the stablehand blushed when he realized she'd understood him.

Beck and Diablo burst into the ring, the animal's hooves kicking up dirt as he tore around in a circle. Mimi whooped as they thundered by.

They were a study in contrasts, the blond man on the ebony horse, the golden angel subduing the devil. She watched in fascination as the horse gradually settled and slowed under Beck's guidance. They trotted out of the ring back to Ashley and the stolid Dodger.

His color was high and his expression gleeful as

he brought the subdued horse alongside Ashley's. The stablehand dropped the bridle and moved away. "Ready?"

"Not for that." She pointed at the sullen Diablo, who looked as if he were dying to take his revenge on the puny human on his back.

"Believe me, Dodger won't pull that stunt. He's a walking couch." He clucked to the horses and they ambled along a riding trail shaded by huge oaks draped in Spanish moss. Once they were out of sight of the stable, Beck guided the horses to a stop. "Come here."

He leaned over his saddle with acrobatic ease and kissed her, his warm mouth moving over hers. She dropped her reins and grabbed his shoulders. Fortunately Dodger didn't take that as a signal to bolt. The air was still and heavy with the rich scent of trees and soil and a blue jay cawed overhead. They were along in paradise, an Adam and Eve complete with their own devil.

And he made his presence known, shuffling Beck away from her. He laughed and handed Ashley her forgotten reins. "Spoilsport."

"Oh, well, so much for my fantasy about making love on horseback."

He laughed harder. "Sorry, the students use these trails. Besides, Diablo is too skittish and Dodger isn't strong enough to bear both of our weights."

She adjusted her helmet. "I see you've already considered the logistics."

"Of course." He ran a gloved finger over her cheek. "Being with you is all I think about. But not just making love. I want to show you all sorts of wonderful things." He gestured to the woods around them. "Like my horses, like this trail. And I want to learn about the things you love, too."

"Teddy will be pleased." She couldn't resist teasing him.

He groaned. "My rival for your affections. Can you forgive me for being an ass?"

"I was flattered." She patted his thigh. "And don't worry, Teddy will come around. Just offer him a sunflower seed."

"The key to his heart. And what is the key to yours?"

She laughed uneasily. Just being himself was enough, and maybe too much. "How about a guided tour of this lovely wilderness? I'm more a city girl, you know."

He recognized her attempt to keep things light and went along with it, moving the horses into a steady walk. "Come on, city girl. I'll show you the wonders of nature."

Beck was a wonder of nature himself, one she was unable to resist.

10

"OH, MY GOSH, that was the most wonderful thing ever!" Ashley jumped off the saddle into Beck's waiting arms. Her eyes were shining, her cheeks flushed with pleasure.

"I'm glad you enjoyed it." He couldn't help himself and kissed her laughing lips. Like the kids he taught, Ashley had been apprehensive at first, but as she and the horse got to know each other, she relaxed and even expressed disappointment when they turned the horses home to the stables. She would have stayed out all day if he'd let her, but he knew she'd be stiff and sore the next day if they did.

"I can't believe how much fun I had." He set her on the ground and her legs wobbled a bit. "Wow. That's a lot of exercise." She tucked her arm through his. "No wonder you have such nice legs, Beck. And a nice ass in those pants," she whispered, pinching his butt cheek through his riding breeches.

Beck heard a funny wheezing sound and turned to see Aunt Mimi choking back laughter. He raised a brow and she quickly patted her chest. "Hay fever."

Hay fever, his ass. Well, at least Ashley liked it. The riding, not his ass. Although he was glad she liked that, too.

"When can we go again?" She unstrapped her helmet and tucked it into a row of cubbies along the stable wall.

"After you give your muscles a few days to recuperate."

"And I thought I was in good shape." She gave him a mock pout and burst into laughter.

He made sure Mimi was out of earshot. "Maybe I can take you for another kind of ride."

"What, in your car?"

"Uh…" He realized she was teasing him and had to kiss her again.

"You're frightening the horses," Mimi called. "Stop playing kissy-face and get that girl some lunch."

Beck looked up in annoyance, but his aunt was right. "Do you want to eat at the club?"

A spark of mischief lit her eyes. "No. This time, it's my turn to treat you to lunch."

BECK WONDERED where on earth Ashley was taking him for lunch. They had driven away from the wide-open spaces of the stable into West Palm Beach. The narrow bungalows were on top of each other, and a mix of tourists and locals strolled along the sidewalks, stopping to consult maps and drinking what looked like iced coffees. He didn't think he'd ever been in this part of town before.

"Almost there." She pointed at the next corner. "Turn right, and it's the first restaurant on the left."

Beck pulled his red convertible into the tiny off-street lot, glad he'd left the truck at home. He hoped his car would be safe in that neighborhood.

Ashley must have read his mind. "Don't worry, Beck. This block's pretty safe during the day, and you'll be able to see your car from the restaurant."

"Never crossed my mind."

She winked at him and hopped out as soon as the top was fastened.

Beck took her hand and escorted her into the tiny storefront restaurant. Sabor de las Islas, the neon sign read—Taste of the Islands. That sounded good—he liked Caribbean food. A bell rang as they stepped inside, and the teenage host greeted them. "Table for two?" That was probably their only open table; the place was packed.

Beck was about to reply in the affirmative when a piercing shriek echoed from the kitchen and a plump middle-aged woman, her salt-and-pepper hair pulled into a bun, sprinted toward them. He shoved Ashley behind him in case the cook was running amok with a carving knife.

Ashley gurgled with laughter and elbowed past him. "Mama Rodríguez!"

The older woman enveloped her in a fierce hug. "*Ay, Ashley, mi preciosa! Mi cielo!*" She peppered her endearments with smacking kisses and unleashed a torrent of Cuban-accented Spanish. Beck, being used to Argentina, only understood about half of it, but to his shock, Ashley replied fluently in the same dialect.

"And who is this young man?" Her friend abruptly switched into English.

Ashley introduced him as her friend, Beck Emery. He was weirdly disappointed at the bland description. It wasn't as if he wanted to be introduced as her boyfriend, or even more mortifying, lover, but still…

"And this is my dear friend Letitia's mother, Señora Magdalena Rodríguez, and her husband, Señor Guillermo Rodríguez." A cheerful gray-haired cook waved at them from the kitchen. "This is their lovely restaurant." The *señora* beamed with pride.

Beck took her hand and bowed over it using his best etiquette. "*Señora,* it is a pleasure." He decided, what the hell, and planted a kiss on the back of her hand.

She giggled, and not to be outdone, yanked him into a hearty hug, kissing him on both cheeks. "*Ay,* Ashley, such a nice young man. Why haven't you brought him before?"

He put his arm around Ashley's shoulders. "Letitia only introduced us a short time ago."

"My Letitia?" Her black eyes sparkled and dimmed.

"She called me this morning about Paolo's father. So ill, poor man. Ah, but you are here today and you will have the best meal of your life." She guided them to a cozy booth for two in the corner and hurried away, yelling instructions to her husband in the kitchen.

Beck took his first deep breath in several minutes. "Wow, I can see where your friend Letitia gets her energy."

"You should see them at the holidays. I need a week to recover." She looked fondly after Señora Rodríguez, though.

"And they took care of you when you were young."

She pointed to the ceiling. "Right above our heads. At first, we lived across the hall from each other in the two little apartments. Once I moved in with Tisha, she and I did our homework in the booth by the kitchen and rolled napkins around silverware, wiped tables, that sort of thing."

Beck tried to compare his childhood with Ashley's and failed. He had worked in the stables to take care of his own ponies, but that was hardly the same thing. Suddenly he felt inconsequential and maybe even unworthy.

Señora Rodríguez brought out two icy glasses with mint sprigs. "Mojitos for you. Now that Ashley is old enough to drink rum."

Ashley rolled her eyes. "I've been old enough for several years now."

Señora Magdalena scoffed. "Eh, you're still a baby.

Now drink, drink." She bustled away and returned with several plates. "Ham *croquetas*—croquettes, in English—*tamales con puerco,* marinated olives and *mariquitas de plátanos*—plantain chips."

Beck barely had room for his drink on the table. "Are they joining us for us lunch?"

She gave him a wry grin. "This is only the appetizer course—just for us."

Uh-oh. Beck was glad he didn't have dinner plans since it looked as if he wouldn't need to eat until tomorrow. More dishes followed—rice with chicken, spicy shredded beef, giant meatballs and grilled fish with garlic and lime. He ate some of everything, the food tasting better than anything he'd eaten in four-star restaurants.

Ashley ate heartily as well, making sensual little moans as she chewed her food. Beck shifted uneasily, the fullness of his stomach quickly joined by fullness slightly south of there. "You have a piece of rice at the corner of your mouth."

Her tongue came out to flick at the grain, and he almost groaned. Unfortunately, Señora Rodríguez arrived with their desserts and caught him gawking. She gave him a sidelong glance and cleared away the dirty dishes.

"*Bien,* we have flan, cake *de mango,* coconut cookies and our house specialty, *tres leche* cake—cake of three milks. And Ashley, please stop in the kitchen before you go. Lalo, Sylvia and Ignacio want to say hello because it has been such a lo-o-ong time since you visited." Mama Rodríguez's guilt trip was quickly spoiled by a wide grin and a pat to Ashley's cheek.

Ashley smiled at her and Letitia's mother quickly kissed her on the forehead. *"Mija preciosa."* She hurried to the kitchen.

Ashley sniffled a bit and Beck took her hand across the table. Señora Rodríguez had called Ashley her precious daughter. "I don't know about you, Ash, but I think I'm going to give my pony a hernia trying to carry me around tomorrow."

He knew he had successfully lightened the mood when she squeezed his hand in return. "Your poor horse definitely won't be happy after you try these desserts. Cuba's main crop is sugarcane, so their desserts come in three categories: sweet, sweeter and make-an-appointment-at-the-dentist-for-your-new-cavities sweet."

Beck laughed and let her feed him bites of each treat. Señora Rodríguez was an obvious romantic, only bringing one fork for the two of them. The three-milks cake was a new favorite for him. "You'll have to bring me this cake, Ash. I think I want it for my birthday."

She tilted her head. "When is your birthday?"

He realized he didn't know hers either. "July second. And yours?"

"November twelfth." They both fell silent. July was four months away and he didn't know if they would still be together. He didn't even know what would happen at the end of the polo tournament. He was supposed to fly to New York to discuss business matters with his mother, and then Diego had asked him to fly to Buenos Aires for a tournament.

He decided not to worry about the future. It would settle itself, as it always did. But the thought of Argentina reminded him of something. "Your friend Letitia is married to Paolo Saavedra de Léon, right?"

"I bet you're wondering why her parents still run this place considering Tisha's married to one of the richest men in Patagonia."

"It did cross my mind," he admitted. They could have hired a hundred people to work here, even to expand into many restaurants across South Florida.

"Because they have their pride. They are happy for Letitia to have married Paolo, but only because she loves him and he loves her. He could have been the richest man in the western hemisphere and they wouldn't have given their blessing to her marriage if there wasn't love between them."

Beck considered that radical idea for a few minutes as he nibbled on a coconut cookie. From what he understood, his parents had been thrown together by their respective families at an early age, leading to their engagement and marriage. They spent most of the year apart, his father on his sailboat in the Caribbean and his mother at their home in the Hamptons. Rumors had circulated about various marital indiscretions, but Beck figured the less he knew, the better. And Beck's cousins had married and divorced several times each, the initial flare of passion quickly burning to ashes. "Some say love and marriage are mutually exclusive."

Ashley shrugged. "If I hadn't known Tisha's family, I would agree. But as you can see—" she gestured at the pass-through kitchen window where Señora Rodríguez was chatting with her husband. She tucked a stray gray curl of hair under his white hat, her affection for him obvious.

"Eh, my favorite song!" Letitia's mother cried, turning up a raucous salsa tune on the radio. *"Bailamos!* Everybody dance!"

And damned if everybody didn't. Tisha's parents burst from the kitchen, executing a complicated salsa move right in the middle of the restaurant. The busboys grabbed the waitresses, some old enough to be their mothers, and even the customers abandoned their meals to shake their rears.

It felt as if he'd fallen into a Broadway musical where the rules of logic and normal behavior were swept away by a catchy tune. It was the most bizarre situation he'd been in for a long time, and he loved it.

He jumped up. "Let's dance."

Ashley protested, but he tugged her to her feet and found she was a very good dancer as well. He'd learned several ballroom-style Latin dances, but this restaurant's version was the real thing. He pulled her tight as she swung dangerously close to a full glass of soda sitting on a nearby table.

"I bet you never figured you'd be salsa-dancing during lunch."

He clutched his stomach in mock pain. "Not the best thing to do on a full stomach."

"But you dance so well. Lessons?"

"Complete with little gray suit and boutonniere."

"All the girls must have been in love with you."

She was only teasing, but he remembered their earlier discussion of love. Seeing Señor and Señora Rodríguez laugh and smile at each other, he might concede Ashley's point. Might. The music stopped and he didn't want to stop dancing. "Come to the Polo Club Ball with me."

"The what?" She gave him a startled look.

He was shocked to find his palms sweating as if he were asking a girl to the senior prom. "After the final polo match next Friday, the club hosts a black-tie formal ball. I want you to be my date."

"Oh." She thought for an agonizing minute. "No, I don't have anything going on next Friday. Black-tie, you said?"

He nodded and wished he had that other guy's soda to moisten his mouth.

She came to a decision and nodded. "Yes, Beck, I'll go to the ball with you."

"Great!" He stared at her with a big dopey grin and the music started again.

"Eh, my *second*-favorite song!" Señora Rodríguez

exclaimed, and the dancing began all over again. Beck held Ashley close despite the fast tempo and never wanted to let her go.

11

A BALLGOWN. Like Cinderella, Sleeping Beauty and Belle from *Beauty and the Beast*, Ashley needed a ballgown. Not a nice suit, not a little black cocktail dress, but a real-life, honest-to-goodness, not-embarrass-herself-or-Beck ballgown.

She watched Teddy roll around in his plastic ball as if his hypnotic, back-and-forth motion would stimulate some great idea. Instead, she was getting a bit motion sick. "Okay, honey, back in your cage you go." She tucked him away with some sunflower seeds in apology before leaving on her daunting shopping expedition. Tisha would have gladly loaned her a gown, but Ashley was ten inches taller and didn't have Tisha's Cuban curves.

She tried the *quinceañera* shop where all the fourteen-year-olds shopped for their debutante dresses, but not surprisingly, skirts that were six feet wide and poofy were not what she had in mind for the Polo Club Ball.

It was a shame she needed a dress so quickly, the proprietress told her. They could have made her a custom dress out of the many gorgeous fabrics they carried—but not in six days.

Ashley took a deep breath and ventured into the pricey boutiques and bridal salons. They, of course, had lovely dresses, but she couldn't justify putting another several thousand dollars on her credit card. One of the younger salesladies, sensing her distress, pulled her aside and mentioned an upscale resale shop where many of the society ladies sent dresses on consignment.

It was better than any other ideas Ashley had, so she found the shop, discreetly tucked away from the main shopping area. She walked in, a small bell jingling overhead.

"Hello." An older woman dressed in a beautiful lilac silk tunic and white full-cut palazzo pants gave her a friendly smile. "How may I help you today?"

Ashley returned her smile. "I am looking for a ballgown."

"Oh, my. Which event?"

Ashley hesitated and the saleslady patted her hand. "Don't worry, dear. I couldn't own a shop like this if I blabbed my clients' business. I need to know so I can help you choose."

"Oh." Ashley relaxed. That made sense. Ashley always needed to know the occasion when helping her own clients with their jewelry choices. "The Bella Florida Polo Club Tournament Ball."

"My goodness, aren't you the lucky girl? Those only happen every few years, and women practically fight to the death to get invitations."

Ashley's stomach flipped. "Really?" And she had almost arrived in a teenage debutante dress.

"Indeed." The shop-owner eyed her figure. "I think we have some things that might work. Make yourself comfortable in the middle changing room and we'll get started."

She did as she was told and the saleslady brought in an armful of dresses—pink, black, red—none of them worked for her. One was too short, one made her look as if she were recovering from the stomach flu and one wasn't special enough. Finally she spotted a blue dress. "How about that one?"

"My assistant acquired it yesterday—it hasn't even made it onto the rack yet." The saleslady unzipped the dress and helped Ashley into it. "Oh, wow."

Wow, indeed. It was made of aquamarine silk and draped gracefully in folds to the floor. The bodice was strapless. Vine-like silver embroidery curved across a wide band below Ashley's breasts, emphasizing her small waist. The skirt skimmed her hips and pooled around her ankles. It had a classical Greek look and Ashley loved it.

"You see a small train, but that shouldn't get in the way of your dancing. Get some silver sandals and put your hair in a fancy updo and you would look wonderful—you wouldn't even need much jewelry."

Ashley slanted her an amused look. Jewelry was the one thing she had plenty of. She twisted her hair on the top of her head and loved how she looked—elegant, polished, put together. Everything she needed to carry off the evening. Her white-gold poppy bracelet tangled briefly in her hair, so she dropped her arm. She tried discreetly to check the price tag, but there wasn't one yet. "How much?"

The shop owner tapped her nails on the counter for a minute. "I'll give you a fifteen-percent discount for buying it so quickly and also because you look wonderful in it." The amount she named was still well into four figures and Ashley's stomach rolled under the beautiful silver embroidery.

"Oh. Oh, my." She bit her lip and blinked, not wanting to stain the blue silk with tears of disappointment.

The shop owner sighed. "I am sorry, my dear, but I can't drop the price any more. This dress would retail for fifteen thousand dollars new."

"No, no. I totally understand." Great, now she was making the poor saleslady feel bad. "I'm a business-woman as well—jewelry design, actually." She thrust out her arm to show off the poppy bracelet. "We have to do what we can to keep our businesses afloat."

"I'm glad you understand. But that is a lovely brace-let—white gold, correct?" She peered at Ashley's favorite bracelet. Ashley unclipped it and handed it to her.

"Yes, entirely made by my own hands. I don't do mass-market work—hard to control quality that way."

"How much would that retail for, if you don't mind my asking?" She held the gold up to the light, obviously enjoying how it sparkled.

Ashley smiled. She'd never tried to sell the design, but she knew how much it should sell for. "About half of what you so kindly were going to price this dress at."

"Half?" The shop owner came to a decision and stared Ashley in the face. "Don't tell the taxman, but I'm going to offer you a barter deal. Sixty-five percent off the dress since I'll include the original fifteen percent we discussed earlier, and you throw in the bracelet. Cash-flow problems?"

"You don't know the half of it."

"Happens to the best of us. The trick is to keep the stock moving—like this gorgeous dress. What do you say?"

Ashley stared at the shop owner in silence. She had enough to buy the gown at sixty-five percent off, but to sell her bracelet? To make herself feel better, she turned to the mirror again. "I really do look great in this, don't I?"

The woman smiled. "Amazing. Your date won't know what hit him."

That was the sales closer for her. She should take selling lessons from this woman. "All right, we have a deal."

"Wonderful." The saleslady starting peeling Ashley out of the dress. "And be sure to give me some of your business cards. Maybe we can do something about your cash flow."

"Thanks." Ashley was sorry to barter her bracelet away, but it was worth it as she imagined Beck's face when he saw her in the gown. This was the only polo club ball she'd ever attend, that was for sure.

"GOOD MORNING, Beckett."

He fought back a groan. His cell phone had been sitting on the stable bench next to him, and he had immediately answered it, hoping it was Ashley. "Morning, Mom." He could practically hear her teeth grinding on the other end of the line. "Mom" was not amused.

"You and your little jokes, Beckett."

He didn't take her bait. "What can I do for you today?" He eyed the saddle on the stand in front of him. Good. Looked like the stirrups and the girth were still firmly attached.

"You can come to work for me. For the family company," she clarified.

Nope, she had it right the first time. Working *for* her, not *with* her. "Mother, we already discussed this. You want to be in charge. You don't like my ideas on moving the firm into the twenty-first century." Hell, as it was, they were barely into the mid-1950s, computers excepted.

"There is nothing wrong with tradition, especially in a family firm," she countered. "I am just a caretaker for the benefit of you and your sons after you."

Ashley flashed to mind. Beck blinked in surprise. He heard the words *sons* and thought of Ashley? Although any child of hers, boy or girl, would be as beautiful, intelligent and kind as his or her mother. He frowned, not wanting to imagine Ashley dating, marrying, making babies with some loser.

"Beck! Did you hear what I said?"

No, he sure hadn't. "Sorry, Mother, I'm checking the stock-market levels."

"Ha! More like checking your polo gear."

Beck looked at the mallet he was inspecting. Busted. "Mother…"

"If you put a fraction of the effort into our business that you put into your horses." He was surprised by the real frustration in her voice. "You are wasting your talents riding around on horses all day and partying all night."

"I am hardly a brainless dilettante, Mother." He had spoken more sharply than he intended and took a deep breath. "I enjoy competing with the Pan-Florida team, I manage my string of ponies and I even donate some time to charity."

"That's not enough. Did it ever occur to you that I am not getting any younger and I need you to learn how to run the firm?"

His mother had plenty of talented executives who could easily step into her shoes. No single one of them could do what she did, but a group definitely could.

"Maybe the firm would be better off without me running it."

"What are you saying, Beckett?" Her voice had become icy.

"I don't know, Mother."

"You'd better figure it out." She cut their connection with a click.

He blew out a sigh and slumped against the wall. His mother loved the firm almost as much as she loved him and possibly more than she loved his father—but since his father loved his sailboat equally, he figured it was a wash. He had been too young to remember all the details, but his mother's brother had almost run the company into the ground, forcing his mother to step in to save it from bankruptcy. The parts Beck did remember were her long hours and preoccupation even when she did make it home.

Was it any wonder he wasn't leaping at the chance to take her place? He shook his head and stood, setting the polo mallet into the rack.

He surveyed the stable and its equipment. Every horse had its place, every mallet and saddle as well. If only life could be so organized and orderly.

ASHLEY OPENED her eyes. She was sunbathing on Beck's pool deck. To her surprise, he enjoyed doing yard work when he was at his villa and was currently mowing the grass bare-chested. He looked hot, hard-bodied and sweaty—a combination she adored.

She decided to distract him from his toil and took off her bikini top. It had been several years since she'd sunbathed topless, and the sun caressed her bare skin.

She deliberately stretched her arms over her head and Beck veered the mower into the mulched border, nearly decapitating several flowering plants.

He cut the engine and strode toward her. "If you wanted my full attention, you certainly have it."

"Now, Beck." She teased him and darted behind the chaise longue, keeping it between them. Her nipples tightened in anticipation. "I'm getting some sun in your nice private backyard."

"And you want to find out how private it is, don't you?"

Her bikini top lay on the slate patio between them. He followed her glance and grabbed it. "Is this what you're looking for?"

"Yes, please." She held out her hand.

He shook his head, dangling the coral-pink nylon from his fingers. "Come get it."

"That's okay, I've got another suit in the house." She made a half-hearted break for it.

He whooped and chased her, the bikini top falling by the wayside. She'd almost made it to the house when he caught her and scooped her up amid her squeals. She pressed herself against him so she wouldn't fall.

He glanced at her slick breasts sticking to his sweaty chest and nodded approvingly. "Nice."

"Put me down, Beck. You're going to give yourself a hernia."

"I'm not gonna drop you, honey." He strode across the patio and stopped at the eight-foot-deep end of the pool, an evil grin on his face.

"Don't you dare, Beck Emery!" She wiggled in his arms, trying to get free.

He smacked her butt, just hard enough to shock her.

"Oh, my God! You spanked me? You'll be sorry—"

Her scolding turned into a scream as he jumped into the pool. She closed her mouth before the water closed over their heads.

He surfaced laughing. She pushed her dripping hair out of her face and lunged for him. "You—you—" she sputtered.

He evaded her easily. "Cooled off any, Ashley?"

"Cooled off? I'll show you cooled off." She dived underwater and grabbed his waistband, tugging his shorts to his knees.

He sank below the surface and pulled her against his chest. Unable to pay him back with a slap to the ass, she settled for a hard pinch.

They broke the surface simultaneously and gasped for air. "Geez, Ash, I think you left a bruise." He grinned and rubbed his butt.

"I can't believe you ruined your shoes."

"Only a spare pair for cutting the grass." He yanked

off his shoes, chucking them away. His long legs kicked free of his shorts, and they floated away like a black jellyfish. "Your turn."

She dived away from him. "Try to catch me."

Unhampered by any clothing, he grabbed her easily. "Gotcha!" His short hair stood up in spikes and his dark-gold eyelashes clumped together. He leered and pressed her against the pool wall. "It seems that I've caught a mermaid. And to think I thought fishing was a bore."

"Is that your fishing rod or are you happy to see me?" His scorching-hot erection prodded her cool thigh.

He stroked her wet hair off her face, making her shudder as he trailed his hand on her neck. "At least you didn't ask if that was the earthworm I used for bait."

"It lured me just fine." Their legs entwined as she wrapped her arms around his shoulders. He held on to the pool's edge with one hand and cupped the nape of her neck with the other.

They floated together in an erotic synchronized swim, their wet lips sliding across each other. He sucked on her earlobe as she gasped for air. Her fingernails dug into the hard muscles of his butt. Her breasts bobbed gently between them in the blue water, his finger tracing one aching nipple, then the other. "So damn sweet." He buried his face in the curve of her neck and slanted the thick head of his penis along the coral Lycra barrier separating them.

She circled her hips against him, trying to get his swollen shaft at the perfect angle. He tried to thrust against her, but the water's resistance slowed his pace and kept pushing him away. "Damn, this deep water isn't working. I need to touch bottom."

"I thought you'd never ask." She grinned at him and shed her swimsuit bottom, chucking it on the pool deck next to his shoes.

"And I don't have a condom in my pocket." They both looked at his waterlogged running shorts. "I wasn't expecting to need one so soon."

"You didn't?" she teased. "You'll know better next time."

"Next time, but what about now?" He cupped her butt and pulled her close. "You make me want to say to hell with it and not use anything?" He slid his fingers over her clitoris.

She found it extremely difficult to be sensible when he slid his bare cock between her thighs, the base of his shaft pressing her clitoris. "Beck." She gasped for breath as he picked up the pace. He'd never rubbed himself there without protection, and his silky skin was heavenly. "You don't really want to do that."

"Oh, yes I do." He closed his eyes and thrust. If she tipped her hips even slightly, he'd enter her. "When you touch me with your hands, I imagine I'm pressing into your hot, wet depths. Nothing between us."

She pushed away from him, shuddering as the water rippled across her aroused flesh. "You almost made me forget. Go check under my towel by that chair."

"Will I be pleasantly surprised?"

"Hurry back." She couldn't wait much longer.

He hauled himself out and squished over to where she'd been relaxing. "Excellent!" He waved a foil packet triumphantly. "You naughty girl. You had this all planned."

"Not all of it. I wasn't expecting you to chase me topless around your yard and dump me into the pool."

"That little sprint of yours was the high point of *my* day, I can assure you." He eased into the pool with uncharacteristic caution, which amused her when she realized that diving into water was a bad idea for a naked, aroused man.

He grimaced at the waist-high water, but swam to the five-foot section and set the packet on the pool's concrete lip. "Come here, honey. I'm ready to fool around."

"Oh, Beck, you say the sweetest things." She fluttered her eyelashes and glided to him. A jet of warm water hit her thigh and she jumped. "What's that?"

"You found a nozzle. Come float on your back. I'll keep you from going under."

"I don't know about that. You're the guy who dropped me into the pool in the first place." Despite her teasing words, she leaned against him, her head sliding across the slick hair on his chest. She kissed his strong jaw.

"And I had you safe the whole time. Trust me, baby. I'd never let you get hurt." His eyes held desire and something deeper, something she hadn't seen before. He blinked and broke eye contact. "Now that is a nice view."

Ashley followed his stare. Her pink-tipped breasts bobbed at the surface, her nipples taut from the cool water. Beck particularly liked her on top. Good exercise for the glutes and thighs. "I've been doing a lot of riding lately."

"And as a horseman, I do appreciate it. Now shift a bit." He supported her upper body and arranged her legs so her feet straddled the nozzle.

The water streamed against her tender cleft, making her moan. The gentle waves lapped at her like Beck's tongue, licking and teasing until she twisted in his arms.

"I thought you might like that. How about this?" He slipped his hands under her arms and cupped her breasts. He circled his thumbs around her nipples, nudging them into a shivery ache.

Her flexing thighs pushed her body into Beck's embrace. He held her tightly and slipped his long finger over her clitoris, spreading her wide to the silvery ribbon of water. His chest rose and fell under her cheek, his breath coming hard and fast. She was in danger of coming hard and fast herself, but she wanted to wait until Beck was inside her.

She spun around in his arms, a tangle-haired mermaid embracing her human lover. Reaching underwater, she gripped his erect penis. The cool water had not interfered with his arousal. She tugged gently on him, guiding him close to the wall nozzle. "Your turn."

He shuddered and closed his eyes as the water hit

him, playing with his hard shaft and heavy testicles. "I never thought I'd let a woman lead me around by my cock."

"I think you like it anyway."

"I think you're right." He thrust into her hand, his skin gliding against her palm. She wanted to throw caution to the wind and have unprotected sex just once, to have his unsheathed heat slide into her damp flesh. He wouldn't resist, judging from his slightly open mouth and choppy breaths.

But sanity reasserted itself and she grabbed the condom from the pool deck. "Put this on. Now."

He complied, tossing the empty packet onto the concrete and pulling her into his arms for a hungry kiss. She clung to his shoulders, grateful that she didn't have to rely on her wobbly knees for support.

Planting his feet firmly on the pool bottom, Beck cupped her bottom in his big hands. "Hang on tight, honey."

She locked her ankles around his waist and moaned as he surged into her. He paused for a second and withdrew slightly, the cool water eddying against her swollen clitoris.

His next powerful thrust lifted her several inches out of the water. "I'm floating away, Beck."

He hooked his fingers over her shoulders. "We can't have that. I'm never letting you go."

She blinked away a sudden tear, grateful that her damp face disguised the salty drop. Maybe he actually meant that, and not only sexually. She was about to ask him when he ground into her, stroking her clitoris with the top of his thick shaft. Lovely liquid tension swirled from where his penis journeyed into her body's inlet.

She leaned forward and kissed him hard, her wet mouth sliding over his. He took her tongue deep inside his mouth, groaning in the back of his throat as she squeezed him tight inside her. He responded by dipping his thumb between their bodies and stroking her tender nub.

She broke free from their kiss, gasping for air. The heat of his body combined with the cool water made her shudder. He ran his tongue around her ear and whispered naughty things, his honeyed drawl unleashing her climax in a wild wave of pleasure. She ground her body against him, hot, wet and abandoned, knowing he wouldn't drop her. His strong fingers dug into her bottom and anchored her safely to him.

Meeting her thrust for thrust, he gritted his teeth and stiffened in release. He rocked beneath her, stopping his caresses only when the last orgasmic ripples subsided.

She clung to him and tried to catch her breath. "Oh, Beck, that was wonderful. I'll never look at a pool the same way."

"Same here." He was panting as if he'd swum the English Channel. "I'll be lucky to get through my daily laps without adding some extra drag in my swim trunks, if you get my drift."

She smiled and kissed his cheek. Ever since she'd

discovered jewelry design, she'd plotted out her life to the extent of digging herself into a rut. Maybe an unscripted summer interlude drifting along with Beck Emery wasn't a bad idea after all.

12

Two DAYS after their skinny-dip, all thoughts of drifting along in the pool had burned away like morning fog. Raoul had finally called her for a meeting—a meeting to take place the very next day. Ashley had flown into action to coordinate security transportation from her bank vault to the Bruguera Boutique in Palm Beach.

She had done everything she could—polished her jewelry, her sales pitch and her nails. She wore a robin's-egg-blue jacket and matching skirt with a gold spiraling choker necklace and a matching bracelet, which was getting quite the workout as she twisted it nervously. She missed her poppy bracelet but it had gone for a good cause. Enough of that.

Ashley placed her hands calmly on the glass conference table where she had set out her jewelry. It was out of her control now.

The small conference room behind the boutique had the same luxurious pale-gray carpeting as the sales floor but had fluorescent lighting instead of the specialized track and halogen spotlights. For security reasons, there were no windows.

"Ah, Señorita Craig!" Enric swept into the room followed by a man who was as slender as Enric was burly. "And this is my right-hand man, Raoul Gutierrez, who has eagerly been looking forward to this meeting."

Sure he had. The ponytailed Raoul wore a long-suffering expression and during his phone conversations with Ashley had barely contained his annoyance at auditioning a new designer, especially one whom Enric had met poolside. He probably assumed she had been sunbathing topless and was auditioning with nipple rings or something tacky like that.

She gave them both her brightest smile anyway and chatted a bit about the upcoming polo semifinals, careful to leave out Beck's name. She didn't want to seem like a hanger-on or groupie.

Raoul wandered over to her jewelry display and stared expressionlessly at her pieces. During a break in the conversation, Ashley tried to engage Raoul by discussing her pieces. She had brought a variety of her best: platinum, silver and various shades of gold, from white to yellow to the reds and greens used more in her floral and fruit designs.

He asked what she thought was important for the upcoming fall fashion collections and made notes, but no comments on her work. She had brought a black-velvet neck mannequin and showed him several necklaces, using her own hands for rings and bracelets. It was times like this when she wished she could afford to hire a hand model so that she could bite her nails.

Enric kept up a running commentary on her pieces, but Ashley wasn't naive enough to think he was being any less critical than Raoul. Business was business, after all, and a new designer represented a calculated risk to his boutique, in money or in reputation.

"So Señorita Craig, you have a very nice collection here. Doesn't she, Raoul?"

Raoul nodded, his face still deadpan.

"And she is an honorary Cuban, no?"

Enric's provocative statement finally broke through Raoul's ennui. *"Cómo?"* He turned to Enric. *"Una cubana?"*

"Of course," Enric blithely continued in Spanish. "She has that same dreadful accent as you."

Ashley fought back a smile at Raoul's affronted look. "I grew up with my adopted parents in West Palm. They own Sabor de las Islas, and I worked there when I was a kid." If these guys didn't buy her jewelry, she'd be back there bussing tables, but that was her problem.

"Sabor de las Islas? Señora Magdalena's place?" Raoul's narrow face brightened. "My grandmother is María Montoya, one of her best friends."

"Oh, Señora Montoya." Ashley did remember her. "She likes *tres leche* cake with toasted coconut on top."

"Yes, but not so much anymore since she has the

diabetes," Raoul explained. He and Ashley commiserated about that nasty disease and found friends in common while Enric watched them like a kindly matchmaking uncle.

"Enric said your designs would appeal to our wealthy Latin-American clients, but I couldn't see how until now—you have a *Cuban* eye for style." That was obviously a great compliment coming from Raoul, so she thanked him profusely.

Enric glanced at his watch. "Raoul, we have that conference call with Paris in a half hour and I need to discuss the numbers with you now."

"Yes, certainly." Raoul turned to her. "Always a pleasure to meet a fellow Cuban, Señorita Craig."

She smiled and shook their hands before packing her jewelry. The security guards took her cases and readied them for escort to the bank vault while she said her goodbyes.

Once she was in her car behind the security team, she let out a squeal of glee. She had to call Tisha with the hopeful news, but the person she really wanted to call was Beck. But deals fell through all the time, and she decided to wait until she had a contract signed, sealed and delivered. She didn't want his pity at a lost opportunity and she sure wouldn't take his money if he offered her any. She didn't even like using his name for a guest pass.

Ashley had seen her mother angle after men for money, gifts or treats, ecstatic one day at her new dress and in despair the next because her current guy had brought carnations instead of roses. Nuts to the sugar-daddy bit—Ashley would take care of Ashley.

BECK WAVED to his teammates and pointed Caesar toward the stables. His head was still full of Ashley all the time, but at least his game had recovered. No more accidents with his polo mallet, although he'd been tempted to rap Diego a couple times during practice.

Beck dismounted from Caesar and patted his neck. Despite his advancing age, Caesar was a formidable pony, intimidating the other horses with his sheer drive and cunning. He handed Caesar off to the groom and saw Mimi waving frantically at him.

He veered in her direction. "Hey, Meem, what's going on?"

"Your parents are here, Beck. I wanted to give you a heads-up."

"They're in Florida? At their villa?" They owned a home ten minutes from his place.

"No, dummy, *here*." She gestured around them. "I don't know what you said to your mother, but she's in high dudgeon."

Her choice of words distracted Beck for a second. He'd never actually heard anyone say that phrase.

Mimi poked him in the chest with the butt of her riding crop. "Make a fast break for the men's locker room, Beck. Not even your mother will follow you there."

"Beckett!"

"Too late." He turned to see his mother striding toward him, alone. His father was probably in the bar.

"You poor chump. If you were that slow on the uptake on the field, you'd be one of the worst players in polo instead of the best." Mimi waved her crop at his mother and beat a hasty retreat for the stables.

"Thanks, I think." He pasted a pleasant expression on his face. "Mother!"

"Beckett." She tipped her cheek for a kiss and gave him one in return. "My, you smell of horse."

"I've been riding hard for an hour. Would you like to wait while I shower and change?"

"No, that's all right." She wrinkled her nose, but whatever strip she was planning to tear off him was more important than his odor.

"And where is Dad?"

"He saw one of his sailing acquaintances and stopped by the lounge." Mother looked around and spotted a bench along the walkway leading to the main clubhouse. "Shall we sit for a minute?"

He followed, knowing she didn't enjoy being around horses after being thrown and injured as a child. "I hope you had a pleasant trip." She was impeccably dressed as usual, this time in a crisp ivory linen tunic and embroidered pants, but even her careful makeup didn't hide the circles under her hazel eyes, the same color as his.

"It was fine." She made a dismissive gesture. "I came to Florida because I wanted to tell you in person: I've had an offer to purchase the company."

"Your company?" He quickly changed his wording when hurt flashed across her face. "Our company?"

"The only one we have. I have been approached by a discount brokerage house. I'm sure you've heard of it." She named a company that advertised heavily using TV ads and Internet popups touting its cheap trading fees.

"Geez, Mother. What does a firm like that want with ours?"

She quirked a blond eyebrow. "Our good name, of course. Beckett Financial Services is one of the grandes dames of American finance, and they want to improve their own image."

"By piggybacking onto ours." Beck clenched his jaw. The discount brokerage often used scantily-clad models and suggestive commercials. While he wasn't a prude by any means, a client's life savings was too important to bandy about like spring-break beer money in nearby Panama City. "Why would you even consider it?"

"Beckett, the deal looks good. And if you are not going to run Beckett Financial Services, we need to decide on a succession plan."

Beck looked at his mother closely. She wasn't bluffing him—she was seriously considering the sale. He noticed the thinning skin and blue veins on the backs of her hands as she clenched the edge of the bench. "What would you do if you did sell? Retire?"

She sighed. "Beck." He started—she hardly ever called him that. "I have been running the firm since you were small. I didn't want to, but the Securities and

Exchange Commission was knocking on the door, and our clients' money was in danger of disappearing like a puff of smoke. Not to mention all our employees' livelihoods. By the time things had turned around, you were older and busy with school and your riding. I missed a good deal of your childhood and I do not want to miss any more of your life—or your children's lives."

That was the second time she had mentioned those hypothetical grandchildren. "When do you need my decision?"

"We start negotiations when I return to New York next week."

"So soon?"

She gave him a sad smile. "I've waited long enough."

13

WITH A HAND from the driver, Ashley emerged from the limo Beck had sent to her apartment. He had apologized over and over about not being able to come for her in person, but his pony Vespasian had stumbled and possibly pulled a tendon during the final match. She didn't mind his dedication to his horses—after all, they had carried Beck and his team to the winners' circle and he owed them the best care possible.

The match had been another heart-pounding test of her endurance. Despite Bootsie's handpats and Mimi's no-nonsense reassurance, Ashley had dug her nails into her palms at every one of Beck's daredevil moves. He was an utterly calculating, utterly fearless player who earned the championship with his blood and sweat.

And here she was, at the ball to meet the prince. She felt regal, a real Cinderella descending from her coach. She hoped it wouldn't turn into a pumpkin.

She didn't see Beck, so she climbed the stairs to

the ballroom to find him. He wasn't there yet, so she selected a champagne flute from a waiter, her heart thumping under the blue silk and silver embroidery.

Ashley turned her back for a second to look for Mimi and Bootsie, but as sure as if he were a magnet and she were metal, Beck Emery dragged her awareness to him, making everyone's head turn as he stood at the ballroom entrance.

Oh, wow. He had changed from his polo gear into a finely cut midnight-black tuxedo that made the other men look as if they bought theirs off a discount-store clearance rack. A blazing white shirt and a scarlet silk pocket square shone against the dark jacket, an obvious homage to his team colors. His hair was slicked back and he looked very chic and intimidating as he scanned the crowd. Yet another facet to this fascinating man.

He turned his head and caught sight of her, and his face softened. Ashley's mouth went dry and she barely breathed as he greeted well-wishers and fans throughout the room. Despite the delay, she had no doubt he was coming for her, as intent on claiming her as he was on claiming his wins on the field.

Finally, he reached where she stood, half-hidden by the pillar. "Ashley, my beauty."

"Beck," she whispered huskily. Like he had earlier, he took her hand and kissed it, his golden gaze never leaving hers. His lips were warm and soft, unlike his hot, burning kisses earlier.

"You look lovely." He straightened up from her hand

but didn't release it, lacing his fingers through hers. "I've been looking forward to our evening together."

"I have, too." More than she had ever looked forward to an evening.

He stared at a waiter, who immediately gave them champagne. "Another toast." He raised his glass. "To Ashley, a vision in blue."

"Thank you." They sipped their champagne, and the heat built in her from the touch of his hand against hers, his body nestling hers against the pillar. They were unnoticed, but would not be for long, here where Beck was a celebrity.

Trying to restrain herself from leaping into his arms, Ashley decided on conversation. She pointed at his red pocket square. "In honor of your team?"

"Correct. The next time we go to a ball, I want you in flame-red silk to match." His voice was velvety soft and seductive again. "Flame-red to match what I wish we could do now."

"The next time?" Didn't they only host these every few years?

He looked startled, as if he'd said more than he'd intended. He set their champagne flutes on a nearby table. "Would you like to dance with me?" He gestured toward the dance floor, where the lights were dimmed and the band members were tuning their instruments.

"I would love to." Ashley took his arm again, nervousness pounding through her. She had studied dance as a child but thumping around in her tap shoes hadn't prepared her for this.

A gray-haired gentleman stepped up to the band-leader's microphone. "As all of you know, my name is Payton Pennington, and I am the current president of the Bella Florida Polo Club. On behalf of the club and all its members, I would like to welcome you to our Polo Tournament Ball."

Ashley and Beck applauded politely with the rest of the crowd. "Watch out—Pugsy can be a bit long-winded," Beck whispered.

"Pugsy?"

He nodded at the distinguished gentleman. "Nobody calls him Payton."

Geez, did anybody have normal names around here? Pugsy did indeed live up to Beck's expectations, thank-ing half of South Florida for their work in putting on the tournament. He finally arrived at presenting the tourna-ment prizes. More polite applause for the runners-up and then it was the moment of glory for Beck and his team.

"And it is my pleasure to present the silver Bella Florida championship cup to Team Pan-Florida, cap-tained by Beckett Emery and ably assisted by Diego Castellano, Marco Ruiz and Jaime Delgado." Ashley clapped hard as Beck and his team went up onstage to accept their prize. They were a handsome crew, and Ashley could hear more than one comment from the women around her. They were welcome to the other men—but Beck was hers.

After several photos, he returned to her carrying the large two-handled cup. "It's beautiful." She couldn't help running her hands over the exquisitely crafted metal.

"You would do better." He leaned over the cup and kissed her. "Besides, you're my silver prize."

Diego plucked the cup from his hands but Beck let it go. "I can't dance holding it, anyway."

Pugsy the microphone hog continued, "And Beckett Emery will do us the honor of opening our ball with the lovely Miss Ashley Craig."

"What?" She gripped his sleeve in panic. "All by ourselves?"

"May I have this dance?" He pried her fingers off his sleeve and laced them through his.

The center of the ballroom was empty, but Beck didn't wait for anyone to join them. At his nod, the band began a lush waltz tune, and he drew Ashley into position, her hand on his shoulder and his on her waist, their other hands clasped together in the air.

"Beck, I don't know how—" she panicked. How embarrassing to stumble around clutching this graceful man, especially with the whole polo club watching. She was way out of her league, despite the dress and jewelry, no matter what the nice lady at the resale shop had said.

"Shhh." Beck cut through the frenzied monologue running through her head. "The ball committee asked me to open the dancing. I said yes, but on one condition: that I pick the lady to accompany me. You are that lady." His thumb slipped between their hands to stroke her palm, his secret touch making her more agitated, not less. "I wouldn't have anyone else. Now come closer."

Ashley hesitated.

"What? I won't bite you." His voice dropped to a husky purr. "At least, not in public."

Wow. His promise dripped sensuality and blew away the rest of her resistance. She moved in closer so her breasts rested against his chest. She was the only one who saw his nostrils flare as her bodice gaped at their contact, the only one who felt the answering heat leap off his body and singe hers.

"Bailamos." He swung her into the one-two-three beat of the waltz. Ashley was too exhilarated to panic anymore. Beck had said exactly what Mama Rodríguez had said as they had exuberantly danced in her café.

But on the dance floor, Beck was her master, controlling her and moving her wherever he wanted to go. After a few seconds, Ashley realized why the waltz had been considered racy in the old days. His thighs scissored between hers; her breasts pressed against his chest. And his gaze, his gaze was practically molten, never leaving hers.

She was dimly aware that other couples had joined them, among them Mimi and an older gentleman, but they were insignificant in the web of desire Beck was spinning as he twirled them around the room. His cologne mixed with her perfume and, augmented with a healthy dose of pure sex, created a heady new scent.

He stopped when the music ended. Chatter rose around them, but they might as well have been alone in their sensual little cocoon.

"Leave with me." His breath was coming as fast as if he'd just played a match, but she knew one little dance couldn't tire out an athlete like him. "Come to my bed."

"When?" Her heart matched his, racing like one of his ponies.

"I want to say now." Wrenching his glance from hers, he looked around the room, aware of the interested glances sent their way. "But give me some time. I don't want to be rude to those who worked so hard for this event."

"You're so sweet." She gave him the world's sappiest smile, but didn't care.

"I'm not sweet." He stared at her mouth. "I'm hungry—hungry for you." Someone stopped them to congratulate Beck on his championship win. Ashley held Beck's arm as they made small talk. She didn't know any of Beck's acquaintances and they obviously wondered who she was. Oh, how she wished Tisha could have come to the ball so she would have someone to talk to.

But Tisha was still in Argentina while Paolo's father recovered from his nasty case of pneumonia. And there was more news, too—Tisha had called this afternoon to tell her that the twins would get a brother or sister next year.

Ashley had a surprising twinge of envy—not for Tisha's fabulous lifestyle or super-rich in-laws, but for her loving husband and adorable children. And after being left by her mother and father, "baby makes three" was something Ashley had never expected to long for.

"MAY I have this dance, Beckett?" Ashley had stepped away to head for the ladies' room and now his mother stood in front of him. She wore a champagne silk strapless dress that matched her hair, along with a beaded short jacket. Underneath her usual perfection, he noticed an unusual nervousness—nervousness he had probably caused.

"Of course, Mother." He took her into his arms, noticing how fragile her bones were under his touch. "Have you been enjoying the ball?"

"Yes, thank you. Congratulations on your win."

"I'm glad you were here to see it." He guided her around the ballroom, his feet automatically falling into a box step.

She laughed, the first one he'd heard in a long time. "I spent most of the time with my eyes closed in fear. You take entirely too many risks, dear."

"Life without risk is no life at all."

"You did inherit something from me, after all." She blinked a couple of times. "I have to admit something, Beckett. I resented my brother for being given the company to run merely because he was a man. I knew what he was doing was wrong and tried to suggest a different path, but no one listened to me. When he failed, I was almost glad. I saw where playing it safe had led us, so I became a risk-taker. The decisions I made in those early years..." She gave a little shudder. "The board of directors and I had several discussions that could only be described as acrimonious."

"Really?" His mother, so calm and collected, had been a maverick CEO?

"Now, once I was proved correct, the BOD settled down. But I can't tell you the sleepless nights, the cases of antacids I went through." She smiled at him. "I'm not telling you this to pressure you. Just so you understand a little more about your mother and your company."

The music ended and his mother squeezed his hand. "Well, Beckett, it looks as if that beautiful girl in blue is here."

She was, and she was smiling tenderly at him. Beck gulped at his gorgeous woman, his chest feeling as if he'd taken a hoof to the solar plexus.

"Beckett?"

He didn't even glance at his mother. "Ummm?"

"We'll talk again later." She sounded as if she wanted to laugh and turned to visit with some friends.

He pushed through the crowd to meet Ashley.

"Was that your mother, Beck?"

"Oh, um, yes." He pressed a kiss to her hand.

"You look like her." Ashley craned her neck, but Beck had had enough chit-chat.

"Come with me." He escorted her out of the ballroom and along the path to the garden bench at the marble fountain. Instead of stopping, he led her onto the darkened lawn and behind the trunk of a huge live oak. "Kiss me, Ashley." Before waiting for her reply, he pulled her close and covered her mouth with his. She eagerly opened under him, her response to him as intoxicating as the first time they kissed.

But kissing wasn't enough. He leaned back on the rough bark and holding Ashley, he nibbled her neck, inhaling the flowery perfume she'd chosen for the evening. "You smell great."

"So do you." She buried her face in his chest and inhaled. "Even when you're sweaty and hot, you smell wonderful. It makes me want to rip your clothes off." His cock stiffened even more as she opened his jacket and rubbed herself on his thin tuxedo shirt.

He cupped her ass through her dress and yanked her against him. "Don't talk like that unless you want me to do something about it right here." He couldn't stop rubbing her butt, the slippery fabric sliding over the firm flesh as he wanted to slide into her.

"Maybe I do," she murmured. "This evening has been so wonderful already. Make it complete for us, Beck. Make love to me, here, now."

He groaned in desperation, a foil packet burning a hole in his pocket. He found the slit in the side of her skirt and slid his hand where the view of her long tanned legs had been teasing him all night.

"Oh, Beck." She closed her eyes and tipped her head up as he massaged her silky skin.

He found something intriguing. "A thong? What color?"

"Silver—to match the dress."

He pulled the front of the thong free and found the treasure she hid underneath. She was soft and wet, enveloping his fingers with her warmth. She gasped as he found her swollen clitoris. "Oh, Beck, yes."

He grinned and increased his pace. She was as responsive as ever. Maybe too responsive—he muffled her moan with a kiss. Her knees buckled and he wrapped his arm around her waist. "Easy, sweetheart. I don't want you to fall."

"You'd never let me do that, would you, Beck?"

"No, never," he vowed. She was his, and he would keep her safe forever.

"Take me, please, Beck." She shuddered in his embrace and he swiftly undid his trousers and rolled on the condom. Mindful of her delicate dress and even more delicate skin, he wrapped his tux jacket around her before pressing her against the tree.

She lifted her skirt high and he entered her with one stroke. They both gasped.

She whimpered his name and caught at his shoulders as he drove into her. "You feel so good—oh—more."

He obliged, careful not to push her too hard into the

tree, but that didn't seem to matter to her as she hooked a long silky leg around his waist. He grabbed her ass and lifted her up and down his shaft. She reached between their bodies and touched her clit. She had never taken charge of her own pleasure like that before, and he almost came.

Fighting for self-control and feeling the beads of sweat popping on his forehead, he mentally recited Caesar's bloodlines, but that didn't help since he was as aroused and out of control as any stallion.

Her finger brushed his cock, and he swallowed a howl. He wanted this to last forever and he wanted to climax. *You could make this last forever,* a little voice whispered in his head. *Ask her to stay with you after the tournament.*

Ashley's nails bit into his shoulder, her breath panting against his cheek. Her pussy squeezed him tightly and she climaxed hard around his cock. It was too much for him and he followed her into the hazy bliss of pure hot, wet flesh where he melted into her and she melted around him.

They stayed together until her leg quivered and he gently withdrew, kissing her forehead. She gazed at him with a look of wonder, as if he'd taken her on a bed of finest silk covered with rose petals instead of wrapped in his tux jacket against a tree. "That was amazing," she breathed.

"For me, too." He helped her straighten her dress and brushed bark bits off his jacket before putting it on. She used a small pocket mirror to fix her lipstick but she couldn't fix the glow of sexual satisfaction that shimmered around her. On the one hand, he wanted to show off that she was his, and on the other hand, he wanted to hide her from the prying eyes of other men.

Ashley picked a strand of silver thread off his lapel, thread from when she had rubbed her breasts over him. He caught her hand and kissed her palm.

She smiled at him a bit nervously. "Beck," she began. "What happens after the tournament?"

"I have a business meeting in New York and then Diego and I may go to Buenos Aires for a tournament."

She blinked a couple times in surprise. "I mean, what happens with you and me?"

"Oh," he replied cautiously. He'd been so consumed with his need for her that he hadn't thought ahead. "We can get together when I come back to town."

"Whenever that may be." Her full lips pursed wryly and she glanced away from him.

Uh-oh. The only promise he'd made was that he wouldn't date any other women while they were together—however long that was. "I'm sure you'll be busy as well since you've been on vacation from your store. Your assistant will be glad to see you back."

Ashley looked away from him. "Oh, yes, my assistant. She's just been swamped."

"Can she manage for another couple days?" In fact, he was planning to take her home with him for the night and make up for his swift performance with hours and hours of lovemaking.

"What are we doing here, Beck? Are you and I just together for a little fun while it lasts?"

"I think we've had lots of fun, Ash." Her cheeks were starting to redden. "Haven't we?"

"Yes, but…"

He put his arm around her shoulders. "Things get messy if you plan too far ahead. It's better just to go with the flow and see where the river of life takes you."

She shook her head. "That only works if you have a lifejacket, not if you're struggling to keep afloat."

"Are you struggling, Ashley?" It was the first time she had ever alluded to her business being in trouble.

"Does it really matter, Beck? After all, we're only together for however long it lasts. My only request is that you let me know when you leave for Bolivia, Brunei or Brussels—wherever you wind up. Now let's rejoin the party. My throat is dry and I'd like another glass of champagne." She turned on her heel and made her way to the ballroom.

"Sure, I'll find you the best." Beck followed her in dismay. He never meant to hurt Ashley, but she was asking more of him than he could give. Was it time to hang up his saddle and settle down?

Diego appeared at the entrance to the ballroom. "Eh, the conquering hero and his lovely lady. People are looking for you to talk about the match, and some British man wants to invite us to a tournament with one of the royal princes."

"Really?" The British were maniacs for polo—it would be the tournament of a lifetime. His heart started to pound in excitement. Polo was in his blood and it always would be.

14

BACK IN THE BALLROOM, Ashley sipped her champagne. Beck had been as good as his word and had supplied her with the very best vintage the bartender found. She thought about making a toast to them, but didn't particularly want to see the look of panic in his eyes again when she mentioned a long-term relationship—in Beck's case, until the next tournament.

Instead, she put a smile on her face and chatted with friends and fans who wanted to congratulate Beck. Since he'd been the star of the tournament, one fan was Enric Bruguera.

She hadn't heard from him since their meeting when he had examined her jewelry. Enric chatted with Beck in his thick Barcelonan Spanish about the match while Ashley did her best to smile pleasantly and not grab the older man by his exquisitely tailored lapels and shake him until he gave her a yes or a no.

Finally, perhaps in response to her mental begging,

he turned to her. "Ah, Señorita Craig, you look even more beautiful than usual. I hope you are enjoying your evening."

"Yes, thank you."

"You know each other?" Beck looked from one to the other.

"We actually met here at the pool after the first match. By some lucky coincidence, she happened to be a jewelry designer, and I happen to own several fine jewelry boutiques." Enric had obviously guessed that she had deliberately set out to meet him, but he didn't seem to mind.

But Beck did. "I hope that wasn't an imposition for you, Señor Bruguera."

Ashley forced her expression to stay pleasant, but it was difficult. "Señor Bruguera admired my bracelet, and we started talking about our mutual industry after that."

"I must tell you, *señorita,* that Raoul was, how do you say, skeptical when I told him about our luncheon together. He thought I had been fooled by a pretty face." He hastened to add, "And although you are pretty, your work is what impressed Raoul at our meeting."

"I'm glad." She gripped the sides of her dress to hide her anxiety. "Have you made a decision yet?"

"Well, I was planning to have Raoul call you Monday. But since we are all here celebrating a magnificent win…"

She caught her breath.

"We should celebrate another—congratulations, Señorita Craig!" He grabbed her and kissed her on both cheeks. "The Bruguera Boutiques would be pleased and honored to carry your jewelry."

"Oh, thank you, Señor Bruguera!" She leaped up and hugged him around his beefy neck. "I can't tell you how much this means to me."

"Please, call me Enric."

"Oh, of course. And I'm Ashley." She couldn't stop hugging the man. If grouchy Raoul had been there as well, she would have kissed his sourpuss too. "Beck, Beck, did you hear? My jewelry is going to be in Enric's lovely boutiques. My designs!" She abandoned Enric and wrapped her arms around Beck. "Oh, my gosh! I can't believe it."

"Neither can I." Beck's arms had automatically come around her, but he wasn't really returning her hug. They parted and she noticed his face had hardened into a cold expression that she had never seen before. She quickly turned to Enric.

"What happens next?" she asked Enric.

"Raoul will send you contracts to read early next week. After the lawyers are happy with the paperwork, we start our relationship. I know you are familiar with the American clientele but I would like you to travel to our boutiques in Barcelona and Nice soon." He made a uniquely Spanish shrug. "The European ladies, they sometimes prefer slightly different styles."

"Oh, my." Ashley grinned like crazy. A steady

contract plus a trip to Europe? She couldn't believe how wonderful it all sounded. It was her dream come true after all these years of generic frozen dinners, cans of soup and cold cereal for dinner. Heck, Teddy got better food than she did. "I'll look for the papers soon," she promised.

"Wonderful." Enric kissed her on each cheek again. "I must tell you, Señorita Ashley, it has been many years since a designer was brave enough to make such arrangements to sell me herself—her designs," he corrected. "And to think you went to all this trouble to get into the Bella Florida Polo Club. *Brava,* Ashley, *brava.*" He gave a little bow and returned to the party.

Ashley had the feeling her party was over. "Beck—"

He kept his tone low to not attract attention in the middle of the ballroom, but his words might as well have been shouted. "So this is why you came here? Not to spend time with your friend, not to watch our polo tournament, but to stalk that man to sell your jewelry?" His voice dripped disdain, as if she were selling gold chains in a tacky sidewalk kiosk.

"Please, Beck, let's talk about this outside." She tried to guide him away from the crowd, but he shook her off. His eyes were cold chips of amber set in his hard golden face.

"No, tell me now." He wouldn't budge.

She took a deep breath and told him how she had been struggling along and how the fire next door was the last straw. He didn't seem to understand her desperation, though.

"Why didn't you tell me that your shop burned down? That your business was in danger of bankruptcy?"

She looked around and saw the other guests beginning to stare in their direction. Beck's mother was making her way toward them, an expression of concern on her face. Probably that Ashley would embarrass her golden boy after his great triumph. But Beck had insisted they air their dirty laundry in public, so if he got a smelly sock slapped across his face, it was his fault.

"Because I was embarrassed, that's why! I was trying to sell lovely, expensive jewelry in a strip mall between a cigar store and an insurance agency, and it wasn't working. I had no idea what to do except go along with Tisha's plan to meet Enric Bruguera at the polo club to look at my designs."

"Ever heard of small business loan assistance?"

"I have tons of assets on paper! But my landlord won't accept a pair of sapphire earrings for rent, and the grocery store doesn't have a precious metals option when the cashier hits the total button." She gestured around the polo club in frustration. "You might be in the same situation some day. How many of your assets are tied up in your horses? If you ever get short on cash, do you plan to give one pony to your accountant and another to your mortgage company?"

"No, of course not!" He shoved his hands in his pockets. "I would have other options."

His mother touched his sleeve. "Beckett, is everything all right?"

"Just a minute, Mother. Ashley has been telling me about how she used me to further her career."

"I have built my career on my own—unlike you, who have inherited everything and earned nothing."

Beck's mother winced but didn't disagree.

She clenched her fists and moved closer, forcing herself not to react to his scent—and the scent of their lovemaking a few minutes ago. How had things come undone so quickly? "You have the option of a rich family who can bail you out of almost anything. I have no parents and the only family I have I borrowed from Letitia. I will not borrow money from her as well."

"Stubborn pride? Is that all that kept you from asking?"

"You talk to me about stubborn pride? You're the one assuming I only spent time with you to get access to some jeweler. That I lured you with wild sex to attend the polo club events." She shook her head. "You must think I'm some kind of scheming slut. My God, Beck, if I were that good an actress I would have gone to Hollywood and not bothered busting my ass at this stupid jewelry thing." Her voice broke at the last few words.

"Ashley…" He reached for her but she backed away.

"No, don't. Let's end *our* business arrangement now. I won't come around here anymore and you won't touch me. That way we have no misunderstandings, all right?"

She reached into her silver purse and handed him her club guest pass. "Please turn that in for me. I got my hair done at the spa a couple times, so you can send the bill for that to my apartment. I'll repay you as soon as possible."

"Oh, no, my dear, please," his mother interjected. "Beckett, this seems like a terrible misunderstanding with your nice young lady."

"Obviously he doesn't think of me that way, but I appreciate the kindness."

Ashley nodded to Mrs. Emery and walked down the stairs to the front portico, where an idle livery driver was more than happy to run her home.

She refused to cry as he settled her into the backseat and drove away from the ball. The clock had struck midnight for Cinderella and it was time to go back to reality.

BECK WAS STILL DUMBFOUNDED as she dashed past him. "Ashley, where are you going?"

"She's leaving you, of course." His mother put her hands on her hips. "Honestly, Beckett, I wonder if the nanny dropped you on your head when you were an infant. It was before nanny cams, so we'll never truly know."

His father had finally realized something was afoot and came up behind his mother. "I say, Beck, what's the brouhaha?"

"Later, Dad." He ran down the stairs and saw her pale

face in the backseat of a town car. He raced after her along the lawn. He tripped over a hidden sprinkler head. "Ow!" The car gained speed and disappeared down the drive. He rolled onto his back, clutching a knee that had already been bruised in the match. He let rip a few more curses, not caring who heard.

Diego loomed over him, the flickering lights making him even more devilish than usual. "What the hell? I can understand you rolling around in the grass with Ashley, but alone? People are gonna get the wrong idea."

"Shut up and help me stand," he gritted out. Diego extended a hand and hauled Beck to his feet. "I need to find Ashley."

"*Sí*, I saw her rushing away. Is she coming back?"

Beck snorted. "She is gone. Permanently gone. She used me to get into the club to meet some hotshot jeweler from Barcelona."

"Oh, Enric Bruguera?"

"You know that son of a bitch?"

Diego shrugged. "All the girls like his jewelry. Not that I've ever bought any. You need *mucho dinero* for that."

"So you'd be okay with a woman using you to better her own career?"

"Amigo, I would be happy to let Ashley Craig use me however she wanted."

With a blistering Spanish curse, Beck dived for his former friend and the men fell to the ground.

"Beck, you maniac! Get the hell off me!" Diego was

laughing his ass off, though, which enraged Beck further. Diego buried his face into Beck's shoulder so he couldn't get in a good punch.

"Let me get at you, you little…" Beck grabbed Diego's shoulders and tried to force him down, but Diego clutched him harder.

"Beckett Emery! Honestly, do I have to turn the hose on you?" His aunt Mimi stood over them, her hands on her hips. His shocked parents and a goggle-eyed crowd had gathered behind her. Beck realized what their little tableau must look like: him in the grass on top of Diego, Diego holding onto him for dear life.

"Ummm…" Beck just knew he was beet-red. The guests behind his aunt giggled and whispered behind their hands. When things couldn't get any worse, the sprinkler head he'd tripped over decided to get its own revenge and promptly fired a jet of water into his face.

"Well, that will cool you off." Mimi shook her head in disgust and turned away. "Hey, haven't you people ever seen a fistfight before? Not much of one, but that's what it was."

Diego finally let go of Beck and fell wheezing on the ground, laughing too hard to breathe. Beck scraped together the shreds of his dignity and struggled to his knees. His father helped him to his feet. "Thanks, Dad."

His father slapped him on the back. "Buck up, champ. It's always darkest before the dawn."

"Beckett, are you hurt?" His mother brushed a wet lock of hair out of his face.

"Just a bruise." Just his pride.

What a humiliating night: finding out Ashley had only been hanging around with him to get access to that Barcelonan jeweler, having her walk out on him when he confronted her, and now the whole polo club thought he and Diego had something on the side. "I'll check on the ponies before I go home."

His dad nodded approvingly, but his mother still wore a frown of concern. "Please, dear, is there anything we can do?"

Surprisingly his father stepped in. "Not now, Madeline. Sometimes a man just needs to have some time alone."

That was good enough to turn her focus to her husband. "Is that why you live on your boat six months out of the year?"

He kissed her forehead. "I'm just waiting for you to join me, Maddy."

"Oh, Preston." His mom melted. "Do you really want me to come sailing with you?"

"Of course. We'll set sail once everything is settled." He gave Beck a pointed stare. "Beck will be fine, won't you?"

"Yes, just fine." He limped toward the stables, knowing he had just lied to his father.

"KNEW I'd find you here."

Beck stopped petting Caesar's muzzle and turned to look over his shoulder at his aunt. "Hey, Mimi."

She stomped toward him. If she cared that her gray silk dress was dragging through the stable's dust, she certainly didn't let on.

"You know, Beck, everyone says you're so smart, but for the life of me I don't know why."

"Mimi, I don't want to be rude—"

"Why not? *I* am."

He snorted. "Okay: butt out."

"No." She stopped beside him, her bright-blue eyes flashing.

"What do you mean, 'no'? You never stick your nose in my business."

"True," she mused. "I leave all that messy emotional stuff to Bootsie—much easier that way. Your mother has tried coaxing you into taking some of the business load off her shoulders, but doesn't want to scare you off. I, however, have no agenda aside from seeing you grow into the man you should be. Beckett, my dear, you have come to what the touchy-feely idiots call a turning point. Are you going to continue your current career path of charming, shallow young man to its inevitable conclusion as an aging roué?"

He winced. "Geez, Mimi."

She shrugged. "At least I didn't say 'dirty old man.'"

"You just did. And I am not shallow."

"No, you're not, but you've done your best to convince the world that you are, and hell if I know why."

"Is that really what people think of me?" He gripped the top rail of Caesar's stall.

"Most of the people we know don't think, Beck. You understand that," Mimi scoffed. "What's important is your family, your friends—and your girlfriend."

"I don't have a girlfriend."

"Not anymore, you don't!" She slugged him in the shoulder. "Tell me, Beck, what did she do that was so unforgivable?"

"She used me to meet Enric Bruguera to sell him her jewelry designs."

"Half the people here use the club to make business contacts. Why was this different?"

"Because…because…" He struggled for words to explain her betrayal.

"Because, you poor sap, you love her."

"Love," he automatically spat.

"Yes, *love*. Don't feel bad. It makes boneheads of us all. Bootsie went overboard with her baker's dozen of husbands, and I drove away the only man who ever loved me." She said that last phrase matter-of-factly. "He wanted to marry me, but I let stupid pride get in my way."

That was the first he'd heard of that, but from the faraway look in Mimi's eyes, it still bothered her.

"Is this the point where you tell me not to repeat your mistakes?"

That wiped the wistful expression from her face, which was his intention. "No, this is the point where

I take my riding crop and beat your ass until the mere sight of a saddle will make you cry." She huffed out an indignant breath. "Don't be a dumbass, Beck. If you can't man up enough to start making a real life for yourself, not even my riding crop will knock any sense into you."

15

"THAT UPTIGHT, rude bastard Beck Emery needs to come down to earth to live with the rest of us mortals." Tisha paced as best as she could in Ashley's living room considering that Ashley was using it as her full jewelry studio. Despite Tisha's long flight from Buenos Aires, she looked surprisingly fresh in a lime-colored tank top and black shorts. Ashley felt haggard in comparison in her old college T-shirt and gray yoga pants.

"Why should he? It probably looks pretty good from there." Ashley stared grimly at the wax carving of a lily-pad brooch she was working on. Fortunately lily-pad leaves were relatively smooth but she did need to add some veining to make it look more realistic. She picked up a small carving knife.

"And you." Tisha whirled to point at her. "Why are you so calm?"

"Because my brand-new lawyer called this morning

to tell me the contracts with Bruguera Boutiques are all signed and legal."

Tisha squealed and dragged Ashley to her feet. She grabbed Ashley's shoulders and hugged her. Ashley tried to hug her back, but wound up doing more of an apathetic pat on the back.

Tisha stopped and peered into Ashley's eyes. "What is wrong with you? You saved your career. Why aren't you happy?"

She shrugged off Tisha's grip and sat at her workbench. "I am. See? That's why I need to get to work." She picked up her knife and started scraping at the lily-pad wax.

"It's him, isn't it?"

"Yes, Enric is a demanding boss, but it's a relief to stop all the hassle of running the shop, paying rent, meeting payroll—"

"Not Enric—that rotten Beck Emery!"

Ashley's embossing tool slipped, gouging a deep groove into the soft wax leaf. "He is not rotten!" Ashley snapped. "He is smart and funny and kind. He even founded that stable for disabled riders—did you know that?"

"What stable?" Tisha wasn't part of the horsy set.

"It's a wonderful stable. They take kids with disabilities and help them ride horses. Oh, Tisha, it was great to see how happy they were. And it was all Beck's doing."

"Why doesn't he say anything about it?" Tisha demanded. "Why keep up the whole playboy act, the whole living-off-mommy's money thing? He must have much more depth to him if you're in love with him."

"Oh, he does—" Ashley started to agree until she heard the last half of Tisha's sentence. "Wait, who said I was in love with him?" Her stomach tightened and she stood up from her bench to stretch it out. "I never said anything about loving him."

Tisha's big brown eyes were full of sympathy. "No, you never did. And I doubt you ever would say anything, so I'm saying it first. You love that man, warts and all."

Ashley's knees weakened and she collapsed on the couch. "I can't love a man after only a couple of weeks with him."

"No, I'd say it was love at first sight." Tisha sat next to her and put her arm around Ashley's shoulders. "*Chica,* I was there when that bolt of lightning struck you two."

A sob ripped from Ashley's depths and she put her fist to her mouth in shock.

Tisha yanked her hand away as if Ashley were one of her toddlers. "Look at you! Your first honest emotion of the day and you are literally stuffing it down. Stop!"

"No. I'm fine." In reality, her living room was blurring as she blinked quickly.

"You are not. What kind of Cuban are you?" Tisha demanded. "Cry! Rage! Throw things—I'll duck. God knows I had enough practice growing up with my mother. Lose your temper! Scream at the sun, howl at the moon."

Ashley shook her head. "I can't."

"Why the hell not?"

Her voice came out in a whisper. "Because I'll shatter into a million pieces with no one to put them together."

"Oh, baby." Tisha's own eyes filled with tears and that was the last straw.

Ashley shattered right there on her couch, sobbing out all her grief and rage. Rage at her father for never bothering to know her. Rage at her mother for knowing her and leaving her anyway. Grief at her lost childhood. Grief for her shop burning up. And most of all, sorrow for falling in love with Beck during that golden time of happy bliss in his arms.

Why couldn't she have admired him from afar on the polo field, as if he were a beautiful statue in the garden? Instead, she'd seen inside his heart, seen his love for his riding students, his affection for Mimi, Bootsie and his mother, his tenderness for Ashley, a woman whom he'd just met, who had used him to further her career.

She cried harder onto Tisha's shoulder, conscious that she was probably leaving a giant splotch of tears. She tried to sit up but Tisha pulled her back. "It's okay, *querida*. You haven't seen boogers until you have two little boys with head colds."

Ashley managed a snuffly laugh, which was Tisha's intent. Tisha stroked her hair as if she were one of her boys. "Ashley, did you ever cry after your mother left?"

She thought for a second. "Once, maybe—when I

found her goodbye note on the kitchen table. After that, no—I didn't want to hurt your mother's feelings by making her think I was unhappy or ungrateful that you had taken me in."

"All those years. Oh, Ash." Her grip tightened. "We assumed you cried in private. It never occurred to Mama that you didn't cry at all."

"Don't tell her." Ashley sat up in alarm.

"No! No more secrets! Enough is enough—with my mother, and with Beck." Tisha made a chopping motion with her hands. "You have always put all your love and passion into your work. Well, gold and silver cannot love you back. Maybe your Beck can."

"You said he was rotten." Ashley was getting confused.

"I don't care if he's so rotten I need to put a clothespin on my nose when you bring him to dinner. If you tell him you love him and he loves you, that is good enough for me."

"I do love him." Ashley looked at her friend in wonder. The shattered pieces were starting to reassemble into someone new and even stronger. The only pieces that refused to come together were the ones where her heart should be. Maybe Beck would help her heart become whole again—maybe he wouldn't. "How is it possible to love someone so quickly?"

"Hey, don't look at me." Tisha shrugged. "I fell in love with Paolo's ass. Lucky for me, his heart and soul were just as fine."

BECK SAT NEXT to his pool wearing only his swim trunks and a grim expression. He stared at the championship cup on his poolside table and sipped a tumbler of whiskey—a double, straight—not on the rocks. The rest of his life was already on the rocks as it was.

The sterling-silver cup shone in the bright sun—like Ashley's dress had shone in the moonlight. He ran a hand over his hair and drained the glass.

How had things gone wrong so quickly? And why did he care? He'd only known Ashley for a grand total of two weeks—not nearly enough time to turn his life upside down.

He'd known plenty of beautiful blondes before, after all. Blondes who hadn't snuggled up to Beck just to make a business deal. Those women hadn't needed to run a business—he doubted if they even could. Not to mention Ashley's amazing talent in taking cold metal and hard stones and turning them into jeweled bits of nature.

But she hadn't needed her own jewelry to shine. She hadn't even worn her favorite poppy bracelet to the dance. Maybe she'd already sold it to that Bruguera. He reached for his laptop, cursing himself for being seven kinds of idiot. But that still didn't stop him from typing Ashley's name into a search engine. She had a well-designed Web site with an announcement of her new affiliation with Bruguera Boutiques. He clicked on her photo and sat there mooning over the tilt of her head, her bright blue eyes and lovely smile.

He forced himself to click away from her Web site and saw a couple of hits on an online auction.

Beck winced, wondering if she had been so desperate as to list some jewelry for sale that way. Her statement that he never had to worry about a cash crunch was right on the money, so to speak.

Was he spoiled? He stared blankly at the computer screen. He thought of his mother, still working her ass off as CEO of his family business with little help from him. He thought of Diego, who despite his freewheeling image, spent more money on his horses' care than he did his own.

And of course, Ashley, who lavished all her love on Teddy, the first and only rodent to inspire jealousy in him. Jealous because she loved the hamster and not him.

He gulped and quickly clicked on the auction link. Holy crap. It was her poppy bracelet. He rapidly scrolled through the listing and found the seller's ID—a clothing store in Palm Beach, not Ashley.

He dialed the store's number and talked to the owner long enough to get directions and a promise not to sell the bracelet before he arrived. But first, he needed to make another phone call.

"Hello, Mother? Yes, I'm fine. I want to talk to you about the company."

"Isn't it beautiful?" The resale shop owner handed Beck Ashley's white-gold poppy bracelet.

Beck couldn't speak for a second so he nodded. He knew it was hers because it was missing the little jewelers mark near the clasp. That was her secret code, she had explained. Items she sold always had her jeweler's mark, a tiny *A* and *C* intertwined. This bracelet didn't have it, so it had to be her own bracelet that she never took off. Not until now. Why the hell would she sell it? He asked a bit more politely.

The shop owner gave him a bland smile. "Maybe she didn't care for it anymore. Styles change, things come in and out of fashion."

Beck looked around the shop. It carried mostly up-scale casual wear but he noticed some designer dresses on a tall chrome rack. "Tell me, do you ever get really beautiful ball gowns in light-blue silk with lots of silver embroidery?"

The light bulb went on over her head. "Ah, yes. We did have one, but it sold the very same day. I imagine a dress like that would look lovely on a tall blond woman."

"Yes, it did." Ashley had sold her bracelet to buy a ball gown. He'd noticed her brief hesitation before accepting his invitation, but had attributed it to nerves at such a grand party. "I'll buy it." He couldn't fix everything but at least he would return her bracelet.

"Don't you want to know how much it is?"

"No, not really." He reached into his wallet for his credit card.

The shop owner shook her head and laughed. "Good

thing for you I'm an honest businesswoman because I know a desperate man when I see one." She quoted him a fair price, which he gladly paid. She wrapped the bracelet. "How did she look in the blue ball gown?"

"Amazing." Beck's heart thumped at the memory. "And then I wrecked everything."

She handed him the white jewelry box topped with a light-blue bow. "I think this will go a long way toward fixing things."

"Do you really think so?" he asked eagerly.

"But you need to talk to her." The woman folded her arms over her chest. "For heaven's sake, don't shove the box at her and say 'Here you go.' If you're going to do that, you may as well save your money and leave the bracelet with me."

He covered the box. "No. She has to have this bracelet, whether or not she forgives me."

"Good. Tell her that." She finally smiled a genuine smile at him, not just a polite saleswoman-to-customer smile. "My goodness, you make a handsome couple."

He impulsively leaned over the counter and gave her a quick kiss on the cheek before hurrying to the door. "I only hope she agrees."

16

ASHLEY SLUMPED on her couch, feeding sunflower seeds to Teddy. He was the only male she wanted to see in the foreseeable future.

A knock sounded at the door. She looked up in surprise. Maybe it was her neighbor, Mrs. Weinstein. She had offered to drop by with some tomatoes.

She checked the peephole from habit and recoiled in shock. What was Beck doing here? Teddy squealed in protest and she carefully loosened her grip on him and put him in his cage.

"Ashley?" he called. "I know you probably don't want to see me, but I found something that belongs to you."

She made a face. She'd probably left something at his house, but she wished he'd throw it in the mail. "All right." She opened the door.

"May I come in, Ashley?" he asked. She looked for a box of her things, although she couldn't imagine what she'd even left there after only two weeks with Beck.

Two weeks that had meant more to her than anything she had ever experienced with another man.

Fighting the lump in her throat, she gestured wordlessly to the couch. He waited for her to sit and join him. She knotted her hands together, torn between wanting to throw herself on him and wanting to throw him out.

To distract herself, she stared at him. He sure did not look his usual immaculate self. He wore a sun-faded blue T-shirt and swim trunks that had once been red but were now more of a pale brick color. His hair was mussed, sticking up in back, and he sported the rattiest black cloth flip-flops she'd seen since her teenage beach-bum years. "What did you bring for me?"

He looked away, as if gathering his thoughts before speaking. When he did, it wasn't at all what she expected. "I have a story to tell you. Once upon a time, there was a handsome, spoiled prince who had everything—friends, fun, ponies and the money to make his life go smoothly. He was riding along without a care in the world when he met a beautiful golden-haired-princess who was much more than the other princesses he had known. She was smart and funny and talented, and she had turned herself into a princess with absolutely no help from anyone else—a self-made princess."

She drew in a quick breath but he continued, "And this princess was hard-working but needed to meet her fairy godfather to make her jewelry dreams come true."

She giggled to hear Enric so described, absolutely sure the Barcelonan would not appreciate it.

"And she did meet the fairy godfather, but the prince got on his high horse because he had not been the one to make all of her dreams come true."

"Oh, Beck." She tried to caress his cheek, but he caught her hand and kissed her palm. He had made different dreams come true for her.

"The prince took a good, hard look at himself and didn't like what he saw. He realized his mother, the queen, had burdened herself with running the kingdom, so he called her to tell her he would step into the royal executive vice presidency. And he told his royal aunt to plan an expansion for the stable because the queen, overjoyed that the useless prince had actually made an effort to do something worthwhile, made a huge donation and was stiff-arming all her friends to do the same."

Ashley laughed. "Wonderful! I know you love that stable better than anything."

"Better than anything, but not better than you." He swallowed hard, his Adam's apple bobbing above his frayed collar.

Had he said he loved her? "What?"

He winced. "I'm screwing this up—the saleslady warned me not to."

"You talked to a saleslady about this?" She gave him a puzzled frown. For a man who was usually so charming and polished, he wasn't making any sense.

He pulled a long white jewelry box out of his shorts

pocket, its blue ribbon slightly crushed. "This is for you."

"Oh. Okay." She was thinking that a gift of jewelry for her was like giving roses to a florist—until she opened the box. "Oh, my gosh. My bracelet." She pulled it out of the box and he helped her fasten it around her wrist. She wiggled her arm a few times, glad of the bracelet's reassuring weight. "How did you find it?"

He sighed. "I have to admit, although it's going to make me look fairly pathetic, I was drinking whiskey by my pool this morning and missing you terribly. I did an Internet search on you and found the bracelet listed for auction by the lady at the resale shop."

"Oh." Her face burned. Princesses did not shop at secondhand clothing stores.

He pulled her into his arms. "If I'd been thinking, I would have bought a dress for you. But I am so honored that you would sell the bracelet you loved the most to go to the ball with me."

"I do love the bracelet, but not as much as I love you." There. She'd said it, and now all she could do was wait.

"Oh, thank God." He kissed her hard, his lips and tongue moving across hers until she thought she'd faint from pleasure. She finally came up for air and thunked his chest until he let her go.

"What?" His worried expression made her heart do flips.

"Let's try again. I tell you I love you and you say…"

"Oh, Ashley, sweetheart, I love you, too." He tried to kiss her again, but she was laughing too joyfully to even pucker. He surrendered to laughter as well, swinging her up and around until her living room spun into a dizzying blur like Teddy in his hamster ball. Despite all the whirling, the shattered pieces that had been her heart clicked into place, tightly soldered together by their love.

Epilogue

"DID YOU have a good birthday, Ashley?" Beck murmured as he nuzzled her neck. His four-hundred-count sheets were a rumpled mess underneath them.

"The best ever." He had taken her to Jardin des Fleurs and had hand-fed her the best French food she'd ever tasted. His constant caresses under the table and his stolen kisses had inflamed them so much that they hadn't made it to dessert. Her flourless chocolate gâteau was sitting on the granite countertop waiting for them to come up for air.

She yawned and stretched, noting how Beck's gaze followed the rise of her naked breasts. She and Beck had been inseparable for over eight months, and their lovemaking got better and more fulfilling each time.

"Good." He cupped a breast in his hand and kissed the tip. She rolled toward him and slid her thigh between his. His cock was hard and eager for her. He caressed her bottom but stopped. "Wait, you're distracting me, just like you distracted me in the restaurant."

She laughed and pushed her hair from her forehead. "Distracted you from what?"

But he was already out of bed and reaching for his pants. Rummaging through a pocket, he pulled out a pale-gray velvet Bruguera Boutique jewelry box. Not a long necklace box, but a small, square box like those they used for rings. He dropped to one knee.

"Oh, my gosh." She bolted upright in bed.

He took her hand in his. "Marry me, Ash. The months since we've met have been the best of my life. I want to live the rest of my years with you—as your husband."

"Yes, of course." She wrapped her arms around his neck and kissed his sweet mouth. He kissed her back, but then lifted his head.

"Don't you want to see the ring first?" He was only half-teasing. "I know you're particular about your jewelry."

"I would wear the ring from a pop can and be proud to be your wife." She leaned forward and kissed his forehead.

Beck's face softened. "You won't have to." He flipped open the box.

"Oh, Beck, it's gorgeous." She looked at her hand with wonder as he slid the ring on her fourth finger. The ring was the eighteen-carat rose gold she loved, formed into a swirling wave to support a brilliant white diamond at least three carats in size.

"Enric designed it, and Raoul had their very best goldsmith create it. I didn't think a bride should have to design her own ring." He kissed her palm. "It was my grandmother's diamond. My mother has been keeping it safe for me all this time."

"I'm touched she thinks highly enough to trust me with it." She turned her hand back and forth the way the brides she'd worked with for years always did—and now it was her turn. "The diamond is lovely, so bright and beautiful."

"Not as bright and beautiful as you." He tossed away the empty ring box and crawled on the bed next to her. "Let me show you how beautiful you are."

"I'll design your wedding band, Beck," she promised. She fell to the bed next to him, eagerly accepting his kisses and caresses before sitting bolt upright in horror. "Beck!"

"What?" He made to tug her down, but she shook him off.

"What will we say when people ask how you proposed?" She took in his hard, naked body. "I'll blush like crazy."

"It'll be our little secret. And when our kids ask, I'll say, 'Go ask your mom.'" He was grinning ear to ear.

"You are terrible!" But she was laughing too hard to worry. He gathered her into a big hug.

Ashley admired the ring over his shoulder for a brief second and dropped her hand. The true jewel was in her arms, not on her finger.

Harlequin offers a romance for every mood!
*See below for a sneak peek
from our paranormal romance line,
Silhouette® Nocturne™.*
*Enjoy a preview of REUNION by USA TODAY
bestselling author Lindsay McKenna.*

Aella closed her eyes and sensed a distinct shift, like movement from the world around her to the unseen world.

She opened her eyes. And had a slight shock at the man standing ten feet away. He wasn't just any man. Her heart leaped and pounded. He reminded her of a fierce warrior from an ancient civilization. Incan? She wasn't sure but she felt his deep power and masculinity.

I'm Aella. Are you the guardian of this sacred site? she asked, hoping her telepathy was strong.

Fox's entire body soared with joy. Fox struggled to put his personal pleasure aside.

Greetings, Aella. I'm the assistant guardian to this sacred area. You may call me Fox. How can I be of service to you, Aella? he asked.

I'm searching for a green sphere. A legend says that the Emperor Pachacuti had seven emerald spheres created for the Emerald Key necklace. He had seven of his priestesses and priests travel the world to hide these spheres from evil forces. It is said that when all seven spheres are found, restrung and worn, that Light will return to the Earth. The fourth sphere is here, at your sacred site. Are you aware of it? Aella held her breath. She loved looking at him, especially his sensual mouth. The desire to kiss him came out of nowhere.

Fox was stunned by the request. *I know of the Emerald Key necklace because I served the emperor at the time it was created. However, I did not realize that one of the spheres is here.*

Aella felt sad. Why? Every time she looked at Fox, her heart felt as if it would tear out of her chest. *May I stay in touch with you as I work with this site?* she asked.

Of course. Fox wanted nothing more than to be here with her. To absorb her ephemeral beauty and hear her speak once more.

Aella's spirit lifted. What *was* this strange connection between them? Her curiosity was strong, but she had more pressing matters. In the next few days, Aella knew her life would change forever. How, she had no idea....

Look for REUNION
by USA TODAY *bestselling author*
Lindsay McKenna,
available April 2010, only from
Silhouette® Nocturne™.

OLIVIA GATES

BILLIONAIRE, M.D.

Dr. Rodrigo Valderrama has it all…
everything but the woman he's secretly
desired and despised. A woman forbidden
to him—his brother's widow.
And she's pregnant.

Cybele was injured in a plane crash
and lost her memory. All she knows is
she's falling for the doctor who has swept her
away to his estate to heal. If only the secrets
in his eyes didn't promise to tear
them forever apart.

Available March wherever you buy books.

Always Powerful, Passionate and Provocative.

SPECIAL EDITION

INTRODUCING A BRAND-NEW MINISERIES FROM *USA TODAY* BESTSELLING AUTHOR

KASEY MICHAELS

SECOND-CHANCE BRIDAL

At twenty-eight, widowed single mother Elizabeth Carstairs thinks she's left love behind forever....until she meets Will Hollingsbrook. Her sons' new baseball coach is the handsomest man she's ever seen—and the more time they spend together, the more undeniable the connection between them. But can Elizabeth leave the past behind and open her heart to a second chance at love?

FIND OUT IN

SUDDENLY A BRIDE

*Available in April
wherever books are sold.*

HARLEQUIN *Presents*

2 Stories in 1

HER MEDITERRANEAN PLAYBOY

Sexy and dangerous—he wants you in his bed!

The sky is blue, the azure sea is crashing
against the golden sand and the sun is hot.

The conditions are perfect for
a scorching Mediterranean seduction
from two irresistible untamed playboys!

Indulge your senses with these two delicious stories

A MISTRESS AT THE ITALIAN'S COMMAND
by *Melanie Milburne*

ITALIAN BOSS, HOUSEKEEPER MISTRESS
by *Kate Hewitt*

Available April 2010 from Harlequin Presents!

COMING NEXT MONTH

Available March 30, 2010

#531 JUST FOOLING AROUND
Encounters
Julie Kenner and Kathleen O'Reilly

#532 THE DRIFTER
Smooth Operators
Kate Hoffmann

#533 WHILE SHE WAS SLEEPING...
The Wrong Bed: Again and Again
Isabel Sharpe

#534 THE CAPTIVE
Blaze Historicals
Joanne Rock

#535 UNDER HIS SPELL
Forbidden Fantasies
Kathy Lyons

#536 DELICIOUSLY DANGEROUS
Undercover Lovers
Karen Anders

www.eHarlequin.com

HBCNMBPA0310